MINLA'S FLOWERS

MINLA'S FLOWERS

ALASTAIR REYNOLDS

Thousandth Night and Minla's Flowers Copyright © 2009 by Alastair Reynolds. All rights reserved.

"Minla's Flowers" Copyright © 2008 by Alastair Reynolds, first appeared in *The New Space Opera*, edited by Gardner Dozois and Jonathan Strahan. All rights reserved.

Dust jacket illustration Copyright © 2009 by Tomislav Tikulin. All rights reserved.

Interior design Copyright © 2009 by Desert Isle Design, LLC. All rights reserved.

First Edition

ISBN
978-1-59606-259-7

Subterranean Press
PO Box 190106
Burton, MI 48519

www.subterraneanpress.com

MINLA'S FLOWERS

*M*ISSION INTERRUPTED.
 I still don't know quite what happened. The ship and I were in routine Waynet transit, all systems ticking over smoothly. I was deep in thought, a little drunk, rubbing clues together like a caveman trying to make fire with rocks, hoping for the spark that would point me toward the gun, the one no one ever thinks I'm going to find, the one I know with every fibre of my existence is out there somewhere.

Then it happened: a violent lurch that sent wine and glass flying across the cabin, a shriek from the ship's alarms as it went into panic mode. I knew right away that this was no ordinary Way turbulence. The ship was tumbling badly, but I fought my way to the command deck and did what I could to bring her back under control. Seat-of-the-pants flying, the way Gallinule and I used to do it on Plenitude, when Plenitude still existed.

That was when I knew we were outside the Waynet, dumped back into the crushing slowness of normal space. The stars outside were stationary, their colors showing no suggestion of relativistic distortion.

"Damage?" I asked.

"How long have you got?" the ship snapped back.

I told it to ease off on the wisecracks and start giving me the bad news. And it most certainly was bad news. The precious syrinx was still functional—I touched it and felt the familiar tremble that indicated it was still sensing the nearby Waynet—but that was about the only flight-critical system that hadn't been buckled or blown or simply wiped out of existence by the unscheduled egress.

We were going to have to land and make repairs. For a few weeks or months—however long it took the ship to scavenge and process the raw materials it needed to fix itself—the search for my gun would be on hold.

That didn't mean I was counting on a long stopover.

THE SHIP STILL had a slow tumble. Merlin squinted against hard white glare as the burning eye of a bright sun hove into view through the windows. It was white, but not killingly so. Probably a mid-sequence star, maybe a late F or early G type. He thought there was a hint of yellow. Had to be pretty close, too.

"Tell me where we are."

"It's called Calliope," *Tyrant* told him. "G-type. According to the last Cohort census the system contained fifteen planet-class bodies. There were five terrestrials, four of which were uninhabitable. The fifth—the farthest from Calliope—was supposedly colonised by humans in the early Flourishing."

Merlin glanced at the census data as it scrolled down the cabin wall. The planet in question was called Lecythus. It was a typical watery terrestrial, like a thousand others in his experience. It even had the almost-obligatory large single moon.

"Been a while, ship. What are the chances of anyone still being down there?"

MINLA'S FLOWERS

"Difficult to say. A later Cohort flyby failed to make contact with the settlement, but that doesn't mean no one was alive. After the emergence of the Huskers, many planetary colonies went to great lengths to camouflage themselves against the aliens."

"So there could still be a welcoming committee."

"We'll see. With your permission, I'll use our remaining fuel to reach Lecythus. This will take some time. Would you like to sleep?"

Merlin looked back at the coffinlike slab of the frostwatch cabinet. He could skip over the days or weeks that it would take to reach the planet, but that would mean subjecting himself to the intense unpleasantness of frostwatch revival. Merlin had never taken kindly to being woken from normal sleep, let alone the deep hibernation of frostwatch.

"Pass on that, I think. I've still got plenty of reading to catch up on."

Later—much later—*Tyrant* announced that they had reached orbit around Lecythus. "Would you like to see the view?" the ship asked, with a playful note in its voice.

Merlin scratched fatigue from his eyes. "You sound like you know something I don't."

Merlin was at first reassured by what he saw. There was blue ocean down there, swatches of green and brown landmass, large islands rather than any major continental masses, cyclonic swirls of water-vapour clouds. It didn't necessarily mean there were still people, but it was a lot more encouraging than finding a cratered, radioactive corpse of a world.

Then he looked again. Many of those green and brown swatches of landmass were surrounded by water, as his first glimpse had indicated. But some of them appeared to be floating above the ocean completely, casting shadows beneath them. His glance flicked to the horizon, where the atmosphere was compressed into a thin bow of pure indigo. He could see the foreshortened shapes of hovering landmasses, turned nearly edge on. The landmasses appeared to be one or two kilometers thick, and they all appeared to be gently curved. Perhaps half were concave in shape, so their edges were slightly upturned. The edges were frosted white, like the peaks of mountain ranges. Some of the concave masses even had little lakes near their centres. The convex masses were all a scorched tawny grey in color, devoid of water or vegetation, save for a cap of ice at their highest point. The largest shapes, convex or concave, must have been hundreds of kilometers wide. Merlin judged that there must have been at least ten kilometers of clear airspace under each piece. A third of the planet's surface was obscured by the floating shapes.

"Any idea of what we're looking at here?" Merlin asked. "This doesn't look like anything in the census."

"I think they built an armored sky around their world," the ship said. "And then something—very probably Husker-level ordnance—shattered that sky."

"No one could have survived through that," Merlin said, feeling a rising tide of sadness. *Tyrant* was clever enough, but there were times—long times—when Merlin became acutely aware of the heartless machine lurking behind the personality. And then he felt very, very alone. Those were the hours when he would have done anything for companionship, including returning to the Cohort and the tribunal that undoubtedly awaited him.

"Someone does appear to have survived, Merlin."

He perked. "Really?"

"It's unlikely to be a very advanced culture: no neutrino or gravimagnetic signatures, beyond those originating from the mechanisms that must still be active inside the sky pieces. But I did detect some very brief radio emissions."

MINLA'S FLOWERS

"What language were they using? Main? Tradespeak? Anything else in the Cohort database?"

"They were using long beeps and short beeps. I'm afraid I didn't get the chance to determine the source of the transmission."

"Keep listening. I want to meet them."

"Don't raise your hopes. If there are people down there, they've been out of contact with the rest of humanity for a considerable number of millennia."

"I only want to stop for repairs. They can't begrudge me that, can they?"

"I suppose not."

Then something occurred to Merlin, something he realised he should have asked much earlier. "About the accident, ship. I take it you know why we were dumped out of the Waynet?"

"I've run a fault-check on the syrinx. There doesn't appear to be anything wrong with it."

"That's not an answer."

"I know." *Tyrant* sounded sullen. "I still don't have an explanation for what went wrong. And I don't like that any more than you do."

TYRANT FELL INTO the atmosphere of Lecythus. The transmissions had resumed, allowing the ship to pinpoint the origin to one of the larger airborne masses. Shortly afterwards, a second source began transmitting from another floating mass, half the size of the first, located three thousand kilometers to the west. The way the signals started and stopped suggested some kind of agonisingly slow communication via radio pulses, one that probably had nothing to do with Merlin's arrival.

"Tell me that's a code in our database," Merlin said.

"It isn't. And the code won't tell us much about their spoken language, I'm afraid."

Up close, the broken edges of the floating mass soared as tall as a cliff. They were a dark, streaked grey, infinitely less regular than they had appeared from space. The edge showed signs of weathering and erosion. There were wide ledges, dizzying promontories, and cathedral-sized shadowed caves. Glinting in the low light of Calliope, ladders and walkways—impossibly thin and spindly scratches of metal—reached down from the icebound upper reaches, following zigzag trajectories that only took them a fraction of the way to the perilous lower lip, where the floating world curved back under itself.

Merlin made out the tiny moving forms of birdlike creatures, wheeling and orbiting in powerful thermals, some of them coming and going from roosts on the lower ledges.

"But that isn't a bird," *Tyrant* said, highlighting a larger moving shape.

Merlin felt an immediate pang of recognition as the image zoomed. It was an aircraft: a ludicrously fragile assemblage of canvas and wire. It had a crescent moon painted on both wings. There'd been a machine not much more advanced than that in the archive inside the Palace of Eternal Dusk, preserved across thirteen hundred years of family history. Merlin had even risked taking it outside once, to see for himself if he had the nerve to repeat his distant ancestor's brave crossing. He still remembered the sting of reprimand when he'd brought it back, nearly ruined.

This aircraft was even flimsier and slower. It was driven by a single chugging propellor rather than a battery of rocket-assisted turbines. It was following the rim of the landmass, slowly gaining altitude. Clearly it intended to make landfall. The air on Lecythus was thicker at sea level than on Plenitude,

MINLA'S FLOWERS

but the little machine must still have been very close to its safe operational ceiling. And yet it would have to climb even higher if it was to traverse the raised rim.

"Follow it," Merlin said. "Keep us astern by a clear two kilometers. And set hull to stealth."

Merlin's ship nosed in behind the struggling aircraft. He could see the single pilot now, goggled and helmeted within a crude-looking bubble canopy. The plane had reached ten kilometers, but it would need to double that to clear the upturned rim. Every hundred meters of altitude gained seemed to tax the aircraft to the limit, so that it climbed, leveled, climbed. It trailed sooty hyphens behind it. Merlin could imagine the sputtering protest from the little engine, the fear in the pilot's belly that the motor was going to stall at any moment.

That was when an airship hoved around the edge of the visible cliff. Calliope's rays flared off the golden swell of its envelope. Beneath the long ribbed form was a tiny gondola, equipped with multiple engines on skeletal outriggers. The airship's nose began to turn, bringing another crescent moon emblem into view. The aircraft lined up with the airship, the two of them at about the same altitude. Merlin watched as some kind of net-like apparatus unfurled in slow motion from the belly of the gondola. The pilot gained further height, then cut the aircraft's engine. Powerless now, it followed a shallow glide path toward the net. Clearly, the airship was going to catch the aircraft and carry it over the rim. That must have been the only way for aircraft to arrive and depart from the hovering landmass.

Merlin watched with a sickened fascination. He'd occasionally had a presentiment when something was going to go wrong. Now he had that feeling again.

Some gust caught the airship. It began to drift out of the aircraft's glide path. The pilot tried to compensate—Merlin could see the play of light shift on the wings as they warped—but it was never going to be enough. Without power, the aircraft must have been cumbersome to steer. The engines on the gondola turned on their mountings, trying to shove the airship back into position.

Beyond the airship loomed the streaked grey vastness of the great cliff.

"Why did he cut the engines..." Merlin breathed to himself. Then, an instant later: "Can we catch up? Can we do something?"

"I'm afraid not. There simply isn't time."

Sickened, Merlin watched as the aircraft slid past the airship, missing the net by a hundred meters. A sooty smear erupted from the engine. The pilot must have been desperately trying to restart the motor. Moments later, Merlin watched as one wingtip grazed the side of the cliff and crumpled instantly, horribly. The aircraft dropped, dashing itself to splinters and shreds against the side of the cliff. There was no possibility that the pilot could have survived.

For a moment Merlin was numb. He was frozen, unsure what to do next. He'd been planning to land, but it seemed improper to arrive immediately after witnessing such a tragedy. Perhaps the thing to do was find an uninhabited landmass and put down there.

"There's another aircraft," *Tyrant* announced. "It's approaching from the west."

Still shaken by what he'd seen, Merlin took the stealthed ship closer. Dirty smoke billowed from the side of the aircraft. In the canopy, the pilot was obviously engaged in a life-or-death struggle to bring his machine to safety. Even as they watched, the engine appeared to slow and then restart.

Something slammed past *Tyrant*, triggering proximity alarms. "Some kind of shell," the ship told Merlin. "I think someone on the ground is trying to shoot down these aircraft."

MINLA'S FLOWERS

Merlin looked down. He hadn't paid much attention to the landmass beneath them, but now that he did—peering through the holes in a quilt of low-lying cloud—he made out the unmistakeable flashes of artillery positions, laid out along the pale scratch of a fortified line.

He began to understand why the airship dared not stray too far from the side of the landmass. Near the cliff, it at least had some measure of cover. It would have been far too vulnerable to the shells in open air.

"I think it's a time to take a stand," he said. "Maintain stealth. I'm going to provide some lift support to that aircraft. Bring us around to her rear and then approach from under her."

"Merlin, you have no idea who these people are. They could be brigands, pirates, anything."

"They're being shot at. That's good enough for me."

"I really think we should land. I'm down to vapour pressure in the tanks now."

"So's that brave fool of a pilot. Just do it."

The aircraft's engine gave out just as *Tyrant* reached position. Taking the controls manually, Merlin brought his ship's nose into contact with the underside of the aircraft's paper-thin fuselage. Contact occurred with the faintest of bumps. The pilot glanced back down over his shoulder, but the goggled mask hid all expression. Merlin could only imagine what the pilot made of the sleek, whale-sized machine now supporting his little contraption.

Merlin's hands trembled. He was acutely aware of how easily he could damage the fragile thing with a miscalculated application of thrust. *Tyrant* was armored to withstand Waynet transitions and the crush of gas giant atmospheres. It was like using a hammer to push around a feather. For a moment, contact between the two craft was lost, and when *Tyrant* came in again it hit the aircraft hard enough to crush the metal cylinder of a spare fuel tank bracketed on under the wing. Merlin winced in anticipation of an explosion—one that would hurt the little airplane a lot more than it hurt *Tyrant*—but the tank must have been empty.

Ahead, the airship had regained some measure of stability. The capture net was still deployed. Merlin pushed harder, giving the aircraft more altitude in readiness for its approach glide. At the last moment he judged it safe to disengage. He steered *Tyrant* away and left the aircraft to blunder into the net.

This time there were no gusts. The net wrapped itself around the aircraft, the soft impact nudging down the nose of the airship. Then the net began to be winched back toward the gondola like a haul of fish. At the same time the airship swung around and began to climb.

"No other planes?" Merlin asked.

"That was the only one."

They followed the airship in. It rose over the cliff, over the ice-capped rim of the aerial landmass, then settled down towards the shielded region in the bowl, where water and greenery had gathered. There was even a wispy layer of cloud, arranged in a broken ring around the shore of the lake. Merlin presumed that the concave shape of the landmass was sufficient to trap a stable microclimate.

By now Merlin had an audience. People had gathered on the gondola's rear observation platform. They wore goggles and gloves and heavy brown overcoats. Merlin caught the shine of glass lenses being pointed at him. He was being studied, sketched, perhaps even photographed.

"Do you think they look grateful?" he asked. "Or pissed off?"

Tyrant declined to answer.

Merlin kept his distance, conserving fuel as best he could as the airship crossed tens of kilometers of arid, gently sloping land.

MINLA'S FLOWERS

Occasionally they overflew a little hamlet of huts or the scratch of a minor track. Presently the ground became soil-covered, and then fertile. They traversed swathes of bleak grey-green grass, intermingled with boulders and assorted uplifted debris. Then there were trees and woods. The communities became more than just hamlets. Small ponds fed rivers that ambled down to the single lake that occupied the landmass's lowest point. Merlin spied waterwheels and rustic-looking bridges. There were fields with grazing animals, and evidence of some tall-chimneyed industrial structures on the far side of the lake. The lake itself was an easy fifty or sixty kilometers wide. Nestled around a natural harbour on its southern shore was the largest community Merlin had seen so far. It was a haphazard jumble of several hundred mostly white, mostly single-storey buildings, arranged with the randomness of toy blocks littering a floor.

The airship skirted the edge of the town and then descended quickly. It approached what was clearly some kind of secure compound, judging by the guarded fence that encircled it. There was a pair of airstrips arranged in a cross formation, and a dozen or so aircraft parked around a painted copy of the crescent emblem. Four skeletal docking towers rose from another area of the compound, stayed by guylines. A battle-weary pair of partially deflated airships was already tethered. Merlin pulled back to allow the incoming craft enough space to complete its docking. The net was lowered back down from the gondola, depositing the airplane—its wings now crumpled, its fuselage buckled—on the apron below. Service staff rushed out of bunkers to untangle the mess and free the pilot. Merlin brought his ship down at a clear part of the apron and doused the engines as soon as the landing skids touched the ground.

It wasn't long before a wary crowd had gathered around *Tyrant*. Most of them wore long leather coats, heavily belted, with the crescent emblem sewn into the right breast. They had scarves wrapped around their lower faces, almost to the nose. Their helmets were leather caps, with long flaps covering the side of the face and the back of the neck. Most of them wore goggles; a few wore some kind of breathing apparatus. At least half the number were aiming barreled weapons at the ship, some of which needed to be set up on tripods, while some even larger wheeled cannons were being propelled across the apron by teams of well-drilled soldiers. One figure was gesticulating, directing the armed squads to take up specific positions.

"Can you understand what he's saying?" Merlin asked, knowing that *Tyrant* would be picking up any external sounds.

"I'm going to need more than a few minutes to crack their language, Merlin, even if it *is* related to something in my database, of which there's no guarantee."

"Fine. I'll improvise. Can you spin me some flowers?"

"Where exactly are you going? What do you mean, *flowers?*"

Merlin paused at the airlock. He wore long boots, tight black leather trousers, a billowing white shirt, and brocaded brown leather waistcoat, accented with scarlet trim. He'd tied back his hair and made a point of trimming his beard. "Where do you think? Outside. And I want some flowers. Flowers are good. Spin me some indigo hyacinths, the kind they used to grow on Springhaven, before the Mentality Wars. They always go down well."

"You're insane. They'll shoot you."

"Not if I smile and come bearing exotic alien flowers. Remember, I did just save one of their planes."

"You're not even wearing armor."

"Armor would really scare them. Trust me, ship: this is the quickest way for them to understand I'm not a threat."

"It's been a pleasure having you aboard," *Tyrant* said acidly. "I'll be sure to pass on your regards to my next owner."

MINLA'S FLOWERS

"Just make the flowers and stop complaining."

Five minutes later Merlin steeled himself as the lock sequenced and the ramp lowered to kiss the ground. The cold hit him like a lover's slap. He heard an order from the soldiers' leader, and the massed ranks adjusted their aim. They'd been pointing at the ship before. Now it was only Merlin they were interested in.

He raised his right hand palm open, the newly spun flowers in his left.

"Hello. My name's Merlin." He thumped his chest for emphasis and said the name again, slower this time. "*Mer-lin*. I don't think there's much chance of you being able to understand me, but just in case…I'm not here to cause trouble." He forced a smile, which probably looked more feral than reassuring. "Now. Who's in charge?"

The leader shouted another order. He heard a rattle of a hundred safety catches being released. Suddenly, the ship's idea of sending out a proctor first sounded splendidly sensible. Merlin felt a cold line of sweat trickle down his back. After all that he had survived so far, both during his time with the Cohort and since he had become an adventuring free agent, it would be something of a letdown to die by being *shot* with a chemically propelled projectile. That was only one step above being mauled and eaten by a wild animal.

Merlin walked down the ramp, one cautious step at a time. "No weapons," he said. "Just flowers. If I wanted to hurt you, I could have hit you from space with charm-torps."

When he reached the apron, the leader gave another order and a trio of soldiers broke formation to cover Merlin from three angles, with the barrels of their weapons almost touching him. The leader—a cruel-looking young man with a scar down the right side of his face—shouted something in Merlin's direction, a word that sounded vaguely like "distal," but which was in no language Merlin recognized. When Merlin didn't move, he felt a rifle jab into the small of his back. "Distal," the man said again, this time with an emphasis bordering on the hysterical.

Then another voice boomed across the apron, one that belonged to a much older man. There was something instantly commanding about the voice. Looking to the source of the exclamation, Merlin saw the wrecked aircraft entangled in its capture net, and the pilot in the process of crawling out from the tangle, with a wooden box in his hands. The rifle stopped jabbing Merlin's back, and the cruel-looking young man fell silent while the pilot made his way over to them.

The pilot had removed his goggles now, revealing the lined face of an older man, his grey-white beard and whiskers stark against ruddy, weatherworn skin. For a moment Merlin felt that he was looking in the mirror at an older version of himself.

"Greetings from the Cohort," Merlin said. "I'm the man who saved your life."

"Gecko," the red-faced man said, pushing the wooden box into Merlin's chest. "Forlorn gecko!"

Now that Merlin had a chance to examine it properly, he saw that the box was damaged, its sides caved in and its lid ripped off. Inside was a matrix of straw padding and a great many shattered glass vials. The pilot took one of these smashed vials and held it up before Merlin's face, honey-colored fluid draining down his fingers.

"What is it?" Merlin asked.

Leaving Merlin to hold the box and flowers, the red-faced pilot pointed angrily towards the wreckage of his aircraft, and in particular at the cylindrical attachment Merlin had taken for a fuel tank. He saw now that the cylinder was the repository for dozens more of these wooden boxes, most of which must have been smashed when Merlin had nudged the aircraft with *Tyrant*.

MINLA'S FLOWERS

"Did I do something wrong?" Merlin asked.

In a flash the man's anger turned to despair. He was crying, the tears smudging the soot on his cheeks. "Tangible," he said, softer now. "All tangible inkwells. Gecko."

Merlin reached into the box and retrieved one of the few intact vials. He held the delicate thing to his eyes. "Medicine?"

"Plastrum," the man said, taking the box back from Merlin.

"Show me what you do with this," Merlin said, as he motioned drinking the vial. The man shook his head, narrowing his wrinkled ice-blue eyes at him as if he thought that Merlin was either stupid or making fun. Merlin rolled up the sleeve of his arm and motioned injecting himself. The pilot nodded tentatively.

"Plastrum," he said again. "Vestibule plastrum."

"You have some kind of medical crisis? Is that what you were doing, bringing medicines?"

"Tangible," the man repeated.

"You need to come with me," Merlin said. "Whatever that stuff is, we can synthesize it aboard *Tyrant*." He held up the intact vial and then placed his index finger next to it. Then he pointed to the parked form of his ship and spread his fingers wide, hoping the pilot got the message that he could multiply the medicine. "One sample," he said. "That's all we need."

Suddenly there was a commotion. Merlin looked around in time to see a girl running across the apron, toward the two of them. In Cohort terms she could only have been six or seven years old. She wore a child's version of the same greatcoat everyone else wore, buckled black boots and gloves, no hat, goggles, or breathing mask. The pilot shouted "Minla" at her approach, a single word that conveyed both warning and something more intimate, as if the older man might have been her father or grandfather. "Minla oak trefoil," the man added, firmly but not without kindness. He sounded pleased to see her, but somewhat less than pleased that she had chosen this exact moment to run outside.

"Spelter Malkoha," the girl said, and hugged the pilot around the waist, which was as high as she could reach. "Spelter Malkoha, ursine Malkoha."

The red-faced man knelt down—his eyes were still damp—and ran a gloved finger through the girl's unruly fringe of black hair. She had a small, monkeylike face, one that conveyed both mischief and cleverness.

"Minla," he said tenderly. "Minla, Minla, Minla." Then what was clearly a rhetorical question: "Gastric spar oxen, fey legible, Minla?"

"Gorse spelter," she said, sounding contrite. And then, perhaps for the first time, she noticed Merlin. For an anxious moment her expression was frozen somewhere between surprise and suspicion, as if he was some kind of puzzle that had just intruded into her world.

"You wouldn't be called Minla, by any chance?" Merlin asked.

"Minla," she said, in barely a whisper.

"Merlin. Pleased to meet you, Minla." And then on a whim, before any of the adults could stop him, he passed her one of the indigo hyacinths that *Tyrant* had just spun for him, woven from the ancient molecular templates in its biolibrary. "Yours," he said. "A pretty flower for a pretty little girl."

"Oxen spray, Minla," the red-faced man said, pointing back to one of the buildings on the edge of the apron. A soldier walked over and extended a hand to the girl, ready to escort her back inside. She moved to hand the flower back to Merlin.

"No," he said, "you can keep it, Minla. It's for you."

She opened the collar of her coat and pushed the flower inside for safekeeping, until only its head was jutting out. The vivid indigo seemed to throw something of its hue onto her face.

"Mer-lin?" asked the older man.

MINLA'S FLOWERS

"Yes."

The man tapped a fist against his own chest. "Malkoha." And then he indicated the vial Merlin was still carrying. "Plastrum," he said again. Then a question, accompanied by a nod towards *Tyrant*. "Risible plastrum?"

"Yes," Merlin said. "I can make you more medicine. *Risible plastrum.*"

The red-faced man studied him for what seemed like many minutes. Merlin opted to say nothing: if the pilot hadn't got the message by now, no further persuasion was going to help. Then the pilot reached down to his belt and unbuttoned the leather holster of a pistol. He removed the weapon and allowed Merlin sufficient time to examine it by eye. The low sun gleamed off an oiled black barrel, inlaid with florid white ornamentation carved from something like whalebone.

"Mer-lin risible plastrum," Malkoha said. Then he waved the gun for emphasis. "Spar apostle."

"Spar apostle," Merlin repeated, as they walked up the boarding ramp. "No tricks."

EVEN BEFORE *TYRANT* had made progress in the cracking of the local language, Merlin had managed to hammer out a deal with Malkoha. The medicine had turned out to be a very simple drug, easily synthesized. A narrow-spectrum ß-lactam antibiotic, according to the ship: exactly the sort of thing the locals might use to treat a gram-positive bacterial infection—something like bacterial meningitis, for instance—if they didn't have anything better.

Tyrant could pump out antibiotic medicine by the hundreds of liters, or synthesize something vastly more effective in equally large quantities. But Merlin saw no sense in playing his most valuable card so early in the game. He chose instead to give Malkoha supplies of the drug in approximately the same dosage and quantity as he must have been carrying when his aircraft was damaged, packaged in similar-looking glass vials. He gave the first two consignments as a gift, in recompense for the harm he was presumed to have done when attempting to save Malkoha, and let Malkoha think that it was all that *Tyrant* could do to make drugs at that strength and quantity. It was only when he handed over the third consignment, on the third day, that he mentioned the materials he needed to repair his ship.

He didn't say anything, of course, or at least nothing that the locals could have understood. But there were enough examples lying around of the materials Merlin needed—metals and organic compounds, principally, as well as water that could be used to replenish *Tyrant*'s hydrogen-fusion tanks—that Merlin was able to make considerable progress just by pointing and miming. He kept talking all the while, even in Main, and did all that he could to encourage the locals to talk back in their own tongue. Even when he was inside the compound, *Tyrant* was observing every exchange, thanks to the microscopic surveillance devices Merlin carried on his person. Through this process, the ship was constantly testing and rejecting language models, employing its knowledge of both the general principles of human grammar and its compendious database of ancient languages recorded by the Cohort, many of which were antecedents of Main itself. Lecythus might have been isolated for tens of thousands of years, but languages older than that had been cracked by brute computation, and Merlin had no doubt that *Tyrant* would get there in the end, provided he gave it enough material to work with.

It was still not clear whether the locals regarded him as their prisoner, or honored guest. He'd made no attempt to leave, and they'd made no effort to prevent him returning to his ship

MINLA'S FLOWERS

when it was time to collect the vials of antibiotic. Perhaps they had guessed that it would be futile to stop him, given the likely capabilities of his technology. Or perhaps they had guessed—correctly, as it happened—that *Tyrant* would be going nowhere until it was repaired and fueled. In any event they seemed less awed by his arrival than intrigued, shrewdly aware of what he could do for them.

Merlin liked Malkoha, even though he knew almost nothing about the man. Clearly he was a figure of high seniority within this particular organization, be it military or political, but he was also a man brave enough to fly a hazardous mission to ferry medicines through the sky, in a time of war. And his daughter loved him, which had to count for something. Merlin now knew that Malkoha was her "spelter" or father, although he did indeed look old enough to have been spaced from her by a further generation.

Almost everything that Merlin did learn, in those early days, was due to Minla rather than the adults. The adults seemed willing to at least attempt to answer his queries, when they could understand what he was getting at. But their chalkboard explanations usually left Merlin none the wiser. They could show him maps and printed historical and technical treatises, but none of these shed any light on the world's many mysteries. Cracking text would take *Tyrant* even longer than cracking spoken language.

Minla, though, had picture books. Malkoha's daughter had taken an obvious liking to Merlin, even though she shared nothing in common. Merlin gave her a new flower each time he saw her, freshly spun from some exotic species in the biolibrary. Merlin made a point of never giving her flowers from a particular world twice, even when she wanted more of the same. He also made a point of always telling her something of the place from where the flowers had come, regardless of her lack of understanding. It seemed to be enough for her to hear the cadences of a story, even if it was in an alien language.

There was not much color in Minla's world, so Merlin's gifts must have had a luminous appeal to them. Once a day, for a few minutes, they were allowed to meet in a drab room inside the main compound. An adult was always stationed nearby, but to all intents and purposes Merlin and the girl were permitted to interact freely. Minla would show Merlin drawings and paintings she had done, or little compositions, written down in labored handwriting in approximately the form of script *Tyrant* had come to refer to as Lecythus A. Merlin would examine Minla's works and offer praise when it was merited.

He wondered why these meetings were allowed. Minla was obviously a bright girl (he could tell that much merely from the precocious manner of her speaking, even if he hadn't had the ample evidence of her drawings and writings). Perhaps it was felt that meeting the man from space would be an important part of her education, one that could never be repeated at a later date. Perhaps she had pestered her father into allowing her to spend more time with Merlin. Merlin could understand that; as a child he'd also formed harmless attachments to adults, often those that came bearing gifts and especially those adults that appeared interested in what he had to show them.

Could there be more than that, though? Was it possible that the adults had decided that a child offered the best conduit for understanding, and that Minla was now their envoy? Or were they hoping to use Minla as a form of emotional blackmail, so that they might exert a subtle hold on Merlin when he decided it was time to leave?

He didn't know. What he was certain of was that Minla's books raised as many questions as they answered, and that simply leafing through them was enough to open windows in his own mind, back into a childhood he'd thought consigned safely

MINLA'S FLOWERS

to oblivion. The books were startlingly similar to the books Merlin remembered from the Palace of Eternal Dusk, the ones he'd used to fight over with his brother. They were bound similarly, illustrated with spidery ink drawings scattered through the text or florid watercolors gathered onto glossy plates at the end of the book. Merlin liked holding the book up to the light of an open window, so that the illustrated pages shone like stained glass. It was something his father had shown him on Plenitude, when he had been Minla's age, and her delight exactly echoed his own, across the unthinkable gulf of time and distance and circumstance that separated their childhoods.

At the same time, he also paid close attention to the what the books had to say. Many of the stories featured little girls involved in fanciful adventures concerning flying animals and other magic creatures. Others had the worthy, overearnest look of educational texts. Studying these latter books, Merlin began to grasp something of the history of Lecythus, at least insofar as it had been codified for the consumption of children.

The people on Lecythus knew they'd come from the stars. In two of the books there were even paintings of a vast spherical spaceship heaving into orbit around the planet. The paintings differed in every significant detail, but Merlin felt sure that he was seeing a portrayal of the same dimly remembered historical event, much as the books in his youth had shown various representations of human settlers arriving on Plenitude. There was no reference to the Waynet, however, or anything connected to the Cohort or the Huskers. As for the locals' theory concerning the origin of the aerial landmasses, Merlin found only one clue. It lay in a frightening sequence of pictures showing the night sky being riven by lavalike fissures, until whole chunks of the heavens dropped out of place, revealing a darker, deeper firmament beyond. Some of the pieces were shown crashing into the seas, raising awesome waves that tumbled over entire coastal communities, while others were shown hovering unsupported in the sky, with kilometers of empty space under them. If the adults remembered that it was alien weaponry that had smashed their camouflaging sky (weapons deployed by aliens that were still *out here*) no hint of that uncomfortable truth was allowed into Minla's books. The destruction of the sky was shown simply as a natural catastrophe, like a flood or volcanic eruption. Enough to awe, enough to fascinate, but not enough to give nightmares.

Awesome it must have been, too. *Tyrant*'s own analysis had established that the aerial landmasses could be put together like a jigsaw. There were gaps in that jigsaw, but most of them could be filled by lifting chunks of land out of the seas and slotting them in place. The inhabited aerial landmasses were all inverted compared to their supposed positions in the original sky, requiring that they must have been flipped over after the shattering. *Tyrant* could offer little guidance for how this could have happened, but it was clear enough that unless the chunks were inverted, life-supporting materials would spill off over the edges and rain down onto the planet again. Presumably the necessary materials had been uplifted into the air when the unsupported chunks (and these must have been pieces that did not contain gravity nullifiers, or which had been damaged beyond the capacity to support themselves) came hammering down.

As to how people had come to the sky in the first place, or how the present political situation had come into being, Minla's texts were frustratingly vague. There were pictures of what were obviously historic battles, fought with animals and gunpowder. There were illustrations of courtly goings-on; princes and kings, balls and regattas, assassinations and duels. There were drawings of adventurers rising on kites and balloons to survey the aerial masses, and later of what were clearly government-sponsored scouting expeditions, employing huge flotillas

MINLA'S FLOWERS

of flimsy-looking airships. But as to exactly why the people in the sky were now at war with the people on the ground, Merlin had little idea, and even less interest. What mattered—the only thing, in fact—was that Minla's people had the means to help him. He could have managed without them, but by bringing him the things he needed they made it easier. And it was good to see other faces again, after so long alone.

One of Minla's books intrigued him even more than all the others. It showed a picture of the starry night, the heavens as revealed after the fall of the camouflaging sky. Constellations had been overlaid on the patterns of stars, with sketched figures overlaying the schematic lines joining the stars. None of the mythical or heroic figures corresponded to the old constellations of Plenitude, but the same archetypal forms were nonetheless present. For Merlin there was something hugely reassuring in seeing the evidence of similar imaginations at work. It might have been tens of thousands of years since these humans had been in contact with a wider galactic civilization; they might have endured world-changing catastrophes and retained only a hazy notion of their origins. But they were still people, and he was among them. There were times, in his long search for the lost weapon that he hoped would save the Cohort, that Merlin had come to doubt whether there was anything about humanity worth saving. But all it took was the look on Minla's face as he presented her with another flower—another relic of some long-dead world—to banish such doubts almost entirely. While there were still children in the universe, and while children could still be enchanted by something as simple and wonderful as a flower, there was still a reason to keep looking, a reason to keep believing.

THE COILED BLACK device had the look of a tiny chambered nautilus, turned to onyx. Merlin pushed back his hair to let Malkoha see that he was aleady wearing a similar unit, then motioned for Malkoha to insert the translator into his own ear.

"Good," Merlin said, when he saw that the other man had pushed the device into place. "Can you understand me now?"

Malkoha answered very quickly, but there was a moment's lag before Merlin heard his response translated into Main, rendered in an emotionally flat machine voice. "Yes. I understand good. How is this possible?"

Merlin gestured around him. They were alone together in *Tyrant*, with Malkoha ready to leave with another consignment of antibiotics. "The ship's been listening in on every conversation I've had with you," Merlin said. "It's heard enough of your language to begin piecing together a translation. It's still rudimentary—there are a lot of gaps the ship still needs to fill—but it will only get better with time, the more we talk."

Malkoha listened diligently as his earpiece translated Merlin's response. Merlin could only guess at how much of his intended meaning was making it through intact.

"Your ship is clever," Malkoha said. "We talk many times. We get good at understanding."

"I hope so."

Malkoha pointed now at the latest batch of supplies his people had brought, piled neatly at the top of the boarding ramp. The materials were unsophisticated in their manufacture, but they could all be reprocessed to form the complicated components *Tyrant* needed to repair itself.

"Metals make the ship good?"

"Yes," Merlin said. "Metals make the ship good."

"When the ship is good, the ship will fly? You will leave?"

"That's the idea."

MINLA'S FLOWERS

Malkoha looked sad. "Where will you go?"

"Back into space. I've been a long time away from my own people. But there's something I need to find before I return to them."

"Minla will be unhappy."

"So will I. I like Minla. She's a clever little girl."

"Yes. Minla is clever. I am proud of my daughter."

"You have every right to be," Merlin said, hoping that his sincerity came across. "I have to start what I finished, though. The ship tells me it'll be flight-ready in two or three days. It's a patch job, but it'll get us to the nearest motherbase. But there's something we need to talk about first." Merlin reached for a shelf and handed Malkoha a tray upon which sat twelve identical copies of the translator device.

"You will speak with more of us?"

"I've just learned some bad news, Malkoha: news that concerns you, and your people. Before I go I want to do what I can to help. Take these translators and give them to your best people—Coucal, Jacana, the rest. Get them to wear them all the time, no matter who they're talking to. In three days I want to meet with you all."

Malkoha regarded the tray of translators with suspicion, as if the ranked devices were a peculiar foreign delicacy.

"What is the bad news, Merlin?"

"Three days isn't going to make much difference. It's better if we wait until the translation is more accurate, then there won't be any misunderstanding."

"We are friends," Malkoha said, leaning forward. "You can tell me now."

"I'm afraid it won't make much sense."

Malkoha looked at him beseechingly. "Please."

"Something is going to come out of the sky," Merlin said. "Like a great sword. And it's going to cut your sun in two."

Malkoha frowned, as if he didn't think he could possibly have understood correctly.

"Calliope?"

Merlin nodded gravely. "Calliope will die. And then so will everyone on Lecythus."

THEY WERE ALL there when Merlin walked into the glass-partitioned room. Malkoha, Triller, Coucal, Jacana, Sibia, Niltava, and about half a dozen more top brass Merlin had never seen before. An administrative assistant was already entering notes into a clattering electromechanical transcription device squatting on her lap, pecking away at its stiff metal input pads with surprising speed. Tea bubbled in a fat engraved urn set in the middle of the table. An orderly had already poured tea into china cups set before each bigwig, including Merlin himself. Through the partition, on the opposite wall of the adjoining tactical room, Merlin watched another orderly make microscopic adjustments to the placement of the aerial landmasses on an equal-area projection map of Lecythus. Periodically, the entire building would rattle with the droning arrival of another aircraft or dirigible.

Malkoha coughed to bring the room to attention. "Merlin has news for us," he said, his translated voice coming through with more emotion than it had three days earlier. "This is news not just for the Skyland Alliance, but for everyone on Lecythus. That includes the Aligned Territories, the Neutrals and yes, even our enemies in the Shadowland Coalition." He beckoned a hand in Merlin's direction, inviting him to stand.

Merlin held up one of Minla's picture books, open at the illustration of constellations in the sky over Lecythus. "What I have to tell you concerns these patterns," he said. "You see

MINLA'S FLOWERS

heroes, animals, and monsters in the sky, traced in lines drawn between the brightest stars."

A new voice buzzed in his ear. He identified the speaker as Sibia, a woman of high political rank. "These things mean nothing," she said patiently. "They are lines drawn between chance alignments. The ancient mind saw demons and monsters in the heavens. Our modern science tells us that the stars are very distant, and that two stars that appear close together in the sky—the two eyes of Prinia the Dragon, for example—may in reality be located at very different distances."

"The lines are more significant than you appreciate," Merlin said. "They are a pattern you have remembered across tens of thousands of years, forgetting its true meaning. They are pathways between the stars."

"There are no pathways in the void," Sibia retorted. "The void is vacuum: the same thing that makes birds suffocate when you suck air out of a glass jar."

"You may think it absurd," Merlin said. "All I can tell you is that vacuum is not as you understand it. It has structure, resilience, its own reserves of energy. And you can make part of it shear away from the rest, if you try hard enough. That's what the Waymakers did. They stretched great corridors between the stars: rivers of flowing vacuum. They reach from star to star, binding together the entire galaxy. We call it the Waynet."

"Is this how you arrived?" Malkoha asked.

"My little ship could never have crossed interstellar space without it. But as I was passing close to your planet—because a strand of the Waynet runs right through this system—my ship encountered a problem. That is why *Tyrant* was damaged; why I had to land here and seek your assistance."

"And the nature of this problem?" the old man pushed.

"My ship only discovered it three days ago, based on observations it had collated since I arrived. It appears that part of the

Waynet has become loose, unshackled. There's a kink in the flow where it begins to drift out of alignment. The unshackled part is drifting towards your sun, tugged toward it by the pull of Calliope's gravitational field."

"You're certain of this?" Sibia asked.

"I've had my ship check the data over and over. There's no doubt. In just over seventy years, the Waynet will cut right through Calliope, like a wire through a ball of cheese."

Malkoha looked hard into Merlin's eyes. "What will happen?"

"Probably very little to begin with, when the Waynet is still cutting through the chromosphere. But by the time it reaches the nuclear-burning core…I'd say all bets are off."

"Can it be mended? Can the Waynet be brought back into alignment?"

"Not using any technology known to my own people. We're dealing with principles as far beyond anything on Lecythus as *Tyrant* is beyond one of your propellor planes."

Malkoha looked stricken. "Then what can we possibly do?"

"You can make plans to leave Lecythus. You have always known that space travel was possible: it's in your history, in the books you give to your children. If you had any doubts, I've shown it to be the case. Now you must achieve it for yourselves."

"In seventy years?" Malkoha asked.

"I know it sounds impossible. But you can do it. You already have flying machines. All you need to do is keep building on that achievement…building and building…until you have the means."

"You make it sound easy."

"It won't be. It'll be the hardest thing you've ever done. But I'm convinced that you can do it, if only you pull together." Merlin looked sternly at his audience. "That means no more wars between the Skylands and the Shadowlands. You don't

MINLA'S FLOWERS

have time for it. From this moment on, the entire industrial and scientific capacity of your planet will have to be directed toward one goal."

"You're going to help us, Merlin?" Malkoha asked. "Aren't you?"

Merlin's throat had become very dry. "I'd like to, but I must leave immediately. Twenty light years from here is a bountiful system known to the Cohort. The great vessels of my people—the swallowships—sometimes stop in this system, to replenish supplies and make repairs. The swallowships cannot use the Way, but they are very big. If I could divert just one swallowship here, it could carry fifty thousand refugees; double that if people were prepared to accept some hardship."

"That's still not many people," Sibia said.

"That's why you need to start thinking about reducing your population over the next three generations. It won't be possible to save everyone, but if you could at least ensure that the survivors are adults of breeding age..." Merlin trailed off, conscious of the dismayed faces looking at him. "Look," he said, removing a sheath of papers from his jacket and spreading them on the table. "I had the ship prepare these documents. This one concerns the production of wide-spectrum antibiotic medicines. This one concerns the construction of a new type of aircraft engine, one that will allow you to exceed the speed of sound and reach much higher altitudes than are now available to you. This one concerns metallurgy and high-precision machining. This one is a plan for a two-stage liquid-fueled rocket. You need to start learning about rocketry *now*, because it's the only thing that's going to get you into space." His finger moved to the final sheet. "This document reveals certain truths about the nature of physical reality. Energy and mass are related by this simple formula. The speed of light is an absolute constant, irrespective of the observer's motion. This diagram shows the presence of emission lines in the spectrum of hydrogen, and a mathematical formula that predicts the spacing of those lines. All this...*stuff*...should help you make some progress."

"Is this all you can give us?" Sibia asked skeptically. "A few pages' worth of vague sketches and cryptic formulae?"

"They're more than most cultures ever get. I suggest you start thinking about them straight away."

"I will get this to Shama," Coucal said, taking the drawing of a jet engine and preparing to slip it into his case.

"Not before everything here is duplicated and archived," Malkoha said warningly. "And we must take pains to ensure none of these secrets fall into Shadowland hands." Then he returned his attention to Merlin. "Evidently, you gave this matter some thought."

"Just a bit."

"Is this the first time you have had to deal with a world such as ours, one that will die?"

"I've had some prior experience of the matter. There was once a world—"

"What happened to the place in question?" Malkoha asked, before Merlin could finish his sentence.

"It died."

"How many people were saved?"

For a moment Merlin couldn't answer. The words seemed to lodge in the back of his throat, hard as pebbles. "There were just two survivors," he said quietly. "A pair of brothers."

THE WALK TO *Tyrant* was the longest he had ever taken. Ever since he had made the decision to leave Lecythus he had rehearsed the occasion in his mind, replaying it time and again.

MINLA'S FLOWERS

He had always imagined the crowd cheering, daunted by the news, but not cowed, Merlin raising his fist in an encouraging salute. Nothing had prepared him for the frigid silence of his audience, their judgemental expressions as he left the low buildings of the compound, their unspoken disdain hanging in the air like a proclamation.

Only Malkoha followed him all the way to *Tyrant*'s boarding ramp. The old soldier had his coat drawn tight across his chest, even though the wind was still and the evening not particularly cold.

"I'm sorry," Merlin said, with one foot on the ramp. "I wish I could stay."

"You seem like two men to me," Malkoha said, his voice low. "One of them is braver than he gives himself credit for. The other man still has bravery to learn."

"I'm not running away."

"But you are running from something."

"I have to go now. If the damage to the Waynet becomes greater, I may not even be able to reach the next system."

"Then you must do what you think is right. I shall be sure to give your regards to Minla. She will miss you very much." Malkoha paused and reached into his tunic pocket. "I almost forgot to give you this. She would have been very upset with me if I had."

Malkoha had given Merlin a small piece of stone, a coin-shaped sliver that must have been cut from a larger piece and then set in colored metal that so that it could be worn around the neck or wrist. Merlin examined the stone with interest, but in truth there seemed nothing remarkable about it. He'd picked up and discarded more beautiful examples a thousand times in his travels. It had been dyed red in order to emphasize the fine grain of its surface: a series of parallel lines like the pages of a book seen end-on, but with a rhythmic structure to the spacing of the lines—a widening and a narrowing—that was unlike any book Merlin had seen.

"Tell her I appreciated it," he said.

"I gave the stone to my daughter. She found it pretty."

"How did you come by it?"

"I thought you were in a hurry to leave."

Merlin's hand closed around the stone. "You're right. I should be on my way."

"The stone belonged to a prisoner of mine, a man named Dowitcher. He was one of their greatest thinkers: a scientist and soldier much like myself. I admired his brilliance from afar, just as I hope he admired mine. One day, our agents captured him and brought him to the Skylands. I played no part in planning his kidnap, but I was delighted that we might at last meet on equal terms. I was convinced that, as a man of reason, he would listen to my arguments and accept the wisdom of defecting to the Skylands."

"Did he?"

"Not in the slightest. He was as firmly entrenched in his convictions as I was in mine. We never became friends."

"So where does the stone come into it?"

"Before he died, Dowitcher found a means to torment me. He gave me the stone and told me that he had learned something of great significance from it. Something that could change our world. Something that had *cosmic* significance. He was looking into the sky when he said that: almost laughing. But he would not reveal what that secret was."

Merlin hefted the stone once more. "I think he was playing games with you, Malkoha."

"That's the conclusion I eventually reached. One day Minla took a shine to the stone—I kept it on my desk long after Dowitcher was gone—and I let her have it."

"And now it's mine."

MINLA'S FLOWERS

"You meant a lot to her, Merlin. She wanted to give you something in return for the flowers. You may forget the rest of us one day, but please don't ever forget my daughter."

"I won"t."

"I'm lucky," Malkoha said, something in his tone easing, as if he was finished judging Merlin. "I'll be dead long before your Waynet cuts into our sun. But Minla's generation won't have that luxury. They know that their world is going to end, and that every year brings that event a year nearer. They're the ones who'll spend their whole lives with that knowledge looming over them. They'll never know true happiness. I don't envy them a moment of their lives."

That was when something in Merlin gave way, some mental slippage that he must have felt coming for many hours without quite acknowledging it to himself. Almost before he had time to reflect on his own words he found himself saying to Malkoha, "I'm staying."

The other man, perhaps wary of a trick or some misunderstanding brought about by the translator, narrowed his eyes. "Merlin?"

"I said I'm staying. I've changed my mind. Maybe it was what I always knew I had to do, or maybe it was all down to what you just said about Minla. But I'm not going anywhere."

"What I said just now," Malkoha said, "about there being two of you, one braver than the other...I know now which man I am speaking to."

"I don't feel brave. I feel scared."

"Then I know it to be true. Thank you, Merlin. Thank you for not leaving us."

"There's a catch," Merlin said. "If I'm going to be any help to you, I have to see this whole thing out."

MALKOHA WAS THE last to see him before he entered frostwatch. "Twenty years," Merlin said, indicating the settings, which had been recalibrated in Lecythus time units. "In all that time, you don't need to worry about me. *Tyrant* will take care of everything I need. If there's a problem, the ship will either wake me or it will send out the proctors to seek assistance."

"You have never spoken of proctors before," Malkoha replied.

"Small mechanical puppets. They have very little intelligence of their own, so they won't be able to help you with anything creative. But you needn't be alarmed by them."

"In twenty years, must we wake you?"

"No, the ship will take care of that as well. When the time is ready, the ship will allow you aboard. I may be a little groggy at first, but I'm sure you'll make allowances."

"I may not be around in twenty years," Malkoha said gravely. "I am sixty years old now."

"I'm sure there's still life left in you."

"If we should encounter a problem, a crisis…"

"Listen to me," Merlin said, with sudden emphasis. "You need to understand one very important thing. I am not a god. My body is much the same as yours, our lifespans very similar. That's the way we did things in the Cohort: immortality through our deeds, rather than flesh and blood. The frostwatch casket can give me a few dozen years over a normal human lifespan, but it can't give me eternal life. If you keep waking me, I won't live long enough to help you when things get really tough. If there is a crisis, you can knock on the ship three times. But I'd urge you not do so unless things are truly dire."

"I will heed your counsel," Malkoha said.

"Work hard. Work harder than you've ever dreamed possible. Time is going to eat up those seventy years faster than you can blink."

MINLA'S FLOWERS

"I know how quickly time can eat years, Merlin."

"I want to wake to rockets and jet aircraft. Anything less, I'm going to be a disappointed man."

"We will do our best not to let you down. Sleep well, Merlin. We will take care of you and your ship, no matter what happens."

Merlin said farewell to Malkoha. When the ship was sealed up he settled himself into the frostwatch casket and commanded *Tyrant* to put him to sleep.

He didn't dream.

NOBODY HE RECOGNIZED was there to greet Merlin when he returned to consciousness. Were it not for their uniforms, which still carried a recognizable form of the Skylanders' crescent emblem, he could easily believe that he had been abducted by forces from the surface. His visitors crowded around his open casket, faces difficult to make out, his eyes watering against the sudden intrusion of light.

"Can you understand me, Merlin?" asked a woman, with a firm clear voice.

"Yes," he said, after a moment in which it seemed as if his mouth were still frozen. "I understand you. How long have I—"

"Twenty years, just as you instructed. We had no cause to wake you."

He pushed himself from the casket, muscles screaming into his brain with the effort. His vision sharpened by degrees. The woman studied him with a cool detachment. She snapped her fingers at someone standing behind her and then passed Merlin a blanket. "Put this around you," she said.

The blanket had been warmed. He wrapped it around himself with gratitude, and felt some of the heat seep into his old bones.

"That was a long one," he said, his tongue moving sluggishly, making him slur his words. "We don't usually spend so long."

"But you're alive and well."

"So it would seem."

"We've prepared a reception area in the compound. There's food and drink, a medical team waiting to look at you. Can you walk?"

"I can try."

Merlin tried. His legs buckled under him before he reached the door. They would regain strength in time, but for now he needed help. They must have anticipated his difficulties, because a wheelchair was waiting at the base of *Tyrant*'s boarding ramp, accompanied by an orderly to push it.

"Before you ask," the woman said, "Malkoha is dead. I'm sorry to have to tell you this."

Merlin had grown to think of the old man as his only adult friend on Lecythus, and had been counting on his being there when he returned from frostwatch. "When did he die?"

"Fourteen years ago."

"Force and Wisdom. It must be like ancient history to you."

"Not to all of us," the woman said sternly. "I am Minla, Merlin. It may be fourteen years ago, but there isn't a day when I don't remember my father and wish he were still with us."

As he was being propelled across the apron, Merlin looked up at the woman's face and compared it against his memories of the little girl he had known twenty years ago. At once he saw the similarity and knew that she was telling the truth. In that moment he felt the first visceral sense of the time that had passed.

"You can't imagine how odd this makes me feel, Minla. Do you remember me?"

"I remember a man I used to talk to in a room. It was a long time ago."

"Not to me. Do you remember the stone?"

MINLA'S FLOWERS

She looked at him oddly. "The stone?"

"You asked your father to give it to me, when I was due to leave Lecythus."

"Oh, that thing," Minla said. "Yes, I remember it now. It was the one that belonged to Dowitcher."

"It's very pretty. You can have it back if you like."

"Keep it, Merlin. It doesn't mean anything to me now, just as it shouldn't have meant anything to my father. I'm embarrassed to have given it to you."

"I'm sorry about Malkoha."

"He died well, Merlin. Flying another hazardous mission for us, in very bad weather. This time it was our turn to deliver medicine to our allies. We were now making antibiotics for all the landmasses in the Skyland alliance, thanks to the process you gave us. My father flew one of the last consignments. He made it to the other landmass, but his plane was lost on the return trip."

"He was a good man. I only knew him a short while, but I think it was enough to tell."

"He often spoke of you, Merlin. I think he hoped you might teach him more than you did."

"I did what I could. Too much knowledge would have overwhelmed you: you wouldn't have known where to start, or how to put the pieces together."

"Perhaps you should have trusted us more."

"You said you had no cause to wake me. Does that mean you made progress?"

"Decide for yourself."

He followed Minla's instruction. The area around *Tyrant* was still recognizable as the old military compound, with many of the original buildings still present, albeit enlarged and adapted. But most of the dirigible docking towers were gone, as were most of the dirigibles themselves. Ranks of new aircraft now occupied the area where the towers and airships had been before, bigger and heavier than anything Merlin had seen before. The swept-back geometry of their wings, the angle of the leading edge, the rakish curve of their tailplanes, all owed something to the shape of *Tyrant* in atmospheric-entry mode. Clearly the natives had been more observant than he'd given them credit for. Merlin knew he shouldn't have been surprised; he'd given them the blueprints for the jet turbine, after all. But it was still something of a shock to see his plans made concrete, so closely to the way he had imagined it.

"Fuel is always a problem," Minla said. "We have the advantage of height, but little else. We rely on our scattered allies on the ground, together with raiding expeditions to Shadowland fuel bunkers." She pointed to one of the remaining airships. "Our cargo dirigibles can lift fuel all the way back to the Skylands."

"Are you still at war?" Merlin asked, though her statement rather confirmed it.

"There was a ceasefire shortly after my father's death. It didn't last long."

"You people could achieve a lot more if you pooled your efforts," Merlin said. "In seventy—make that fifty—years—you're going to be facing collective annihilation. It isn't going to make a damned bit of difference what flag you're saluting."

"Thank you for the lecture. If it means so much to you, why don't you fly down to the other side and talk to them?"

"I'm an explorer, not a diplomat."

"You could always try."

Merlin sighed heavily. "I did try once. Not long after I left the Cohort...there was a world named Exoletus, about the same size as Lecythus. I thought there might be something on Exoletus connected with my quest. I was wrong, but it was reason enough to land and try and talk to the locals."

"Were they at war?"

MINLA'S FLOWERS

"Just like you lot. Two massive power blocs, chemical weapons, the works. I hopped from hemisphere to hemisphere, trying to play the peacemaker, trying to knock their heads together to make them see sense. I laid the whole cosmic perspective angle on them: how there was a bigger universe out there, one they could be a part of if they only stopped squabbling. How they were going to have to be a part of it whether they liked it or not, when the Huskers came calling, but if they could only be ready for that—"

"It didn't work."

"I made things twenty times worse. I caught them at a time when they were inching towards some kind of ceasefire. By the time I left, they were going at it again hell-for-leather. Taught me a valuable lesson, Minla. It isn't my job to sprinkle fairy dust on a planet and get everyone to live happily ever after. No one gave me the tool kit for that. You have to work these things out for yourself."

She looked only slightly disappointed. "So you'll never try again?"

"Burn your fingers once, you don't put them into the fire twice."

"Well," Minla said, "before you think too harshly of us, it was the Skylands that took the peace initiative in the last ceasefire."

"So what went wrong?"

"The Shadowlands invaded one of our allied surface territories. They were interested in mining a particular ore, known to be abundant in that area."

Depressed as he was by news that the war was still rumbling on, Merlin forced his concentration back onto the larger matter of preparations for the catastrophe. "You've done well with these aircraft. Doubtless you'll have gained expertise in high-altitude flight. Have you gone transonic yet?"

"In prototypes. We'll have an operational squadron of supersonic aircraft in the air within two years, subject to fuel supplies."

"Rocketry?"

"That too. It's probably easier if I show you."

Minla let the orderly wheel him into one of the compound buildings. A long window ran along one wall, overlooking a larger space. Though the interior had been enlarged and re-partitioned, Merlin still recognized the tactical room. The old wall-map, with its cumbersome push-around plaques, had been replaced by a clattering electromechanical display board. Operators wore headsets and sat at desks behind huge streamlined machines, their grey metal cases ribbed with cooling flanges. They were staring at small flickering slate-blue screens, whispering into microphones.

Minla removed a tranche of photographs from a desk and passed them to Merlin for his inspection. They were black-and-white images of the Skyland airmass, shot from increasing altitude, until the curve of Lecythus's horizon became pronounced.

"Our sounding rockets have penetrated to the very edge of the atmosphere," Minla said. "Our three-stage units now have the potential to deliver a tactical payload to any unobstructed point on the surface."

"What would count as a 'tactical payload'?" Merlin asked warily.

"It's academic. I'm merely illustrating the progress we've made in your absence."

"I'm cheered."

"You encouraged us to make these improvements," Minla said chidingly. "You can hardly blame us if we put them to military use in the meantime. The catastrophe—as you've so helpfully pointed out—is still fifty years in the future. We have our own affairs to deal with in the meantime."

MINLA'S FLOWERS

"I wasn't trying to create a war machine. I was just giving you the stepping stones you needed to get into space."

"Well, as you can doubtless judge for yourself, we still have a distance to go. Our analysts say that we'll have a natural satellite in orbit within fifteen years, maybe ten. Definitely so by the time you wake from your next bout of sleep. But that's still not the same as moving fifty thousand people out of the system, or however many it needs to be. For that we're going to need more guidance from you, Merlin."

"You seem to be doing very well with what I've already given you."

Minla's tone, cold until then, softened perceptibly. "We'll get you fed. Then the doctors would like to look you over, if only for their own notebooks. We're glad to have you back with us, Merlin. My father would have been so happy to see you again."

"I'd like to have spoken with him again."

After a moment, Minla said: "How long will you stay with us, until you go back to sleep again?

"Months, at least. Maybe a year. Long enough to know that you're on the right track, and that I can trust you make to your own progress until I'm awake again."

"There's a lot we need to talk about. I hope you have a strong appetite for questions."

"I have a stronger appetite for breakfast."

Minla had him wheeled out of the room into another part of the compound. There he was examined by Skyland medical officials, a process that involved much poking and prodding and whispered consultation. They were interested in Merlin not just because he was a human who had been born on another planet, but because they hoped to learn some secret of frostwatch from his metabolism. Then they were done and Merlin was allowed to wash, clothe himself, and finally eat.

Skyland food was austere compared to what he was used to aboard *Tyrant*, but in his present state he would have wolfed down anything.

There was to be no rest for him that day. More medical examinations followed, including some that were clearly designed to test the functioning of his nervous system. They poured cold water into his ears, shone lights into his eyes, and tapped him with various small hammers. Merlin endured it all with stoic good grace. They would find nothing odd about him because in all significant respects he was biologically identical to the people administering the examinations. But he imagined the tests would give the medical staff much to write about in the coming months.

Minla was waiting for him afterward, together with a roomfull of Skyland officials. He recognized two or three of them as older versions of people he had already met, grayed and lined by twenty years of war—there was Triller, Jacana, and Sibia, Triller now missing an eye—but most of the faces were new to him. Merlin took careful note of the newcomers: those would be the people he'd be dealing with next time.

"Perhaps we should get to business," Minla said, with crisp authority. She was easily the youngest person in the room, but if she didn't outrank everyone present, she at least had their tacit respect. "Merlin, welcome back to the Skylands. You've learned something of what has happened in your absence: the advances we've made, the ongoing condition of war. Now we must talk about the future."

Merlin nodded agreeably. "I'm all for the future."

"Sibia?" Minla asked, directing a glance at the older woman.

"The industrial capacity of the Skylands, even when our surface allies are taken into account, is insufficient for the higher purpose of safeguarding the survival of our planetary culture," Sibia answered, sounding exactly as if she was reading from a strategy document, even though she was looking Merlin straight in the eye. "As such, it is our military duty—our moral imperative—to bring all of Lecythus under one authority, a single Planetary Government. Only then will we have the means to save more than a handful of souls."

"I agree wholeheartedly," Merlin said. "That's why I applaud your earlier ceasefire. It's just a pity it didn't last."

"The ceasefire was always fragile," Jacana said. "The wonder is that it lasted as long as it did. That's why we need something more permanent."

Merlin felt a prickling sensation under his collar. "I guess you have something in mind."

"Complete military and political control of the Shadowlands," Sibia replied. "They will never work with us, unless they become us."

"You can't believe how frightening that sounds."

"It's the only way," Minla said. "My father's regime explored all possible avenues to find a peaceful settlement, one that would allow our two blocs to work in unison. He failed."

"So instead you want to crush them into submission."

"If that's what it takes," Minla said. "Our view is that the Shadowland administration is vulnerable to collapse. It would only take a single clear-cut demonstration of our capability to bring about a coup, followed by a negotiated surrender."

"And this clear-cut demonstration?"

"That's why we need your assistance, Merlin. Twenty years ago, you revealed certain truths to my father." Before he could say anything, Minla produced one of the sheets Merlin had given to Malkoha and his colleagues. "It's all here in black-and-white. The equivalence of mass and energy. The constancy of the speed of light. The interior structure of the atom. Your remark that our sun contains a 'nuclear-burning core.' All these things were a spur to us. Our best minds have grappled with the implications of these ideas for twenty years. We see how the energy of the atom could carry us into space, and beyond range of our sun. We now have an inkling of what else they imply."

"Do tell," Merlin said, an ominous feeling in his belly.

"If mass can be converted into energy, than the military implications are startling. By splitting the atom, or even forcing atoms to merge, we believe that we can construct weapons of almost incalculable destructive force. The demonstration of one of these devices would surely be enough to collapse the Shadowland administration."

Merlin shook his head slowly. "You're heading up a blind alley. It isn't possible to make practical weapons using atomic energy. There are too many difficulties."

Minla studied him with an attentiveness that Merlin found quite unsettling. "I don't believe you," she said.

"Believe me or don't believe me, it's up to you."

"We are certain that these weapons can be made. Our own research lines would have given them to us sooner or later."

Merlin leaned back in his seat. He knew when there was no point in maintaining a bluff.

"Then you don't need me."

"But we do. Most urgently. The Shadowland administration also has its bright minds, Merlin. Their interest in those ore reserves I mentioned earlier…either there have been intelligence links, or they have independently arrived at similar conclusions to us. They are trying to make a weapon."

"You can't be sure of that."

"We can't afford to be wrong. We may own the sky, but our situation is dependent upon access to those fuel reserves. If one of our allies was targeted with an atomic weapon…" Minla left the sentence unfinished, her point adequately made.

"Then build your bomb," Merlin said.

─────── MINLA'S FLOWERS ───────

"We need it sooner rather than later. That is where you come in." Now Minla produced another sheet of paper, flicking it across the table in Merlin's direction. "We have enough of the ore," she said. "We also have the means to refine it. This is our best guess for a design."

Merlin glanced at the illustration long enough to see a complicated diagram of concentric circles, like the plan for an elaborate garden maze. It was intricately annotated in machine-printed Lecythus B.

"I won't help you."

"Then you may as well leave us now," Minla said. "We'll build our bomb in our own time, without your help, and use it to secure peace for the whole world. Maybe that will happen quickly enough that we can begin redirecting the industrial effort towards the evacuation. Maybe it won't. But what happens will be on our terms, not yours."

"Understand one thing," Jacana said, with a hawkish look on his face. "The day will come when atomic weapons are used. Left to our own devices, we'll build weapons to use against our enemy below. But by the time we have that capability, they'll more than likely have the means to strike back, if they don't hit us first. That means there'll be a series of exchanges, an escalation, rather than a single decisive demonstration. Give us the means to make a weapon now and we'll use it in such a way that the civilian casualties are minimized. Withhold it from us, and you'll have the blood of a million dead on your hands."

Merlin almost laughed. "I'll have blood on my hands because I *didn't* show you to kill yourselves?"

"You began this," Minla said. "You already gave us secret knowledge of the atom. Did you imagine we were so stupid, so childlike, that we wouldn't put two and two together?"

"Maybe I thought you had more common sense. I was hoping you'd develop atomic rockets, not atomic bombs."

"This is our world, Merlin, not yours. We only get one chance at controlling its fate. If you want to help us, you must give us the means to overwhelm the enemy."

"If I give you this, millions will die."

"A billion will perish if Lecythus is not unified. You must do it, Merlin. Either you side with us, to the full extent, or we all die."

Merlin closed his eyes, wishing a moment alone, a moment to puzzle over the ramifications. In desperation, he saw a possible solution: one he'd rejected before but was now willing to advance. "Show me the military targets on the surface that you would most like to eradicate," he said. "I'll have *Tyrant* take them out, using charm-torps."

"We've considered asking for your direct military assistance," Minla said. "Unfortunately, it doesn't work for us. Our enemy already know something of your existence: it was always going to be a difficult secret to hide, especially given the reach of the Shadowlander espionage network. They'd be impressed by your weapons, that much we don't doubt. But they also know that our hold on you is tenuous, and that you could just as easily refuse to attack a given target. For that reason you do not make a very effective deterrent. Whereas if they knew that *we* controlled a devastating weapon..." Minla looked at the other Skyland officials. "There could be no doubt in their minds that we might do the unthinkable."

"I'm really beginning to wonder whether I shouldn't have landed on the ground instead."

"You'd be sitting in a very similar room, having a very similar conversation," Minla said.

"Your father would be ashamed of you."

Minla's look made Merlin feel as if he was something she'd found under her shoe. "My father meant well. He served his people to the best of his abilities. But he had the luxury of knowing he was going to die before the world's end. I don't."

MINLA'S FLOWERS

MERLIN WAS ABOARD *Tyrant*, alone except for Minla, while he prepared to enter frostwatch again. Eight frantic months had passed since his revival, with the progress attaining a momentum of its own that Merlin felt sure would carry through to his next period of wakefulness.

"I'll be older when we meet again," Minla said. "You'll barely have aged a day, and your memories of this day will be as sharp as if it happened yesterday. Is that something you ever get used to?"

Not for the first time, Merlin smiled tolerantly. "I was born on a world not very different from Lecythus, Minla. We didn't have landmasses floating through the sky, we didn't have global wars, but in many respects we were quite alike. Everything that you see here—this ship, this frostwatch cabinet, these souvenirs—would once have seemed unrecognizably strange to me. I got used to it, though. Just as you'd get used to it, if you had the same experiences."

"I'm not so sure."

"I am. I met a very intelligent girl twenty years ago, and believe me, I've met some intelligent people in my time." Merlin brightened, remembering the thing he'd meant to show Minla. "That stone you had your father give me...the one we talked about just after I came out of the cabinet?"

"The worthless thing Dowitcher convinced my father was of cosmic significance?"

"It wasn't worthless to you. You must have liked it, or you wouldn't have given it to me in return for my flowers."

"The flowers," Minla said thoughtfully. "I'd almost forgotten them. I used to look forward to them so much, the sound of your voice as you told me stories I couldn't understand but which still managed to sound so significant. You made me feel special, Merlin. I'd treasure the flowers afterwards and go to sleep imagining the strange, beautiful places they'd come from. I'd cry when they died, but then you'd always bring new ones."

"I used to like the look on your face."

"Tell me about the stone," she said, after a silence.

"I had *Tyrant* run an analysis on it. Just in case there was something significant about it, something neither you, I, nor your father had spotted."

"And?" Minla asked, with a note of fearfulness.

"I'm afraid it's just a piece of whetstone."

"Whetstone?"

"Very hard. It's the kind you use for sharpening knives. It's a common enough kind of stone on a planet like this one, wherever you have tides, shorelines, and oceans." Merlin had fished out the stone earlier; now he held it in his hand, palm open, like a lucky coin. "You see that fine patterning of lines? This kind of stone was laid down in shallow tidal water. Whenever the sea rushed in, it would carry a suspension of silt that would settle out and form a fine layer on the surface of the stone. The next time the tide came in, you'd get a second layer. Then a third, and so on. Each layer would only take a few hours to be formed, although it might take hundreds of millions of years for it to harden into stone."

"So it's very old."

Merlin nodded. "Very old indeed."

"But not of any cosmic significance."

"I'm sorry. I just thought you might want to know. Dowitcher *was* playing a game with your father after all. I think Malkoha had more or less guessed that for himself."

For a moment Merlin thought that his explanation had satisfied Minla, enabling her to shut tight that particular chapter of her life. But instead she just frowned. "The lines aren't regular, though. Why do they widen and then narrow?"

"Tides vary," Merlin said, suddenly feeling himself on less solid ground. "Deep tides carry more sediment. Shallow tides less. I suppose."

"Storms raise high tides. That would explain the occasional thick band. But other than that, the tides on Lecythus are very regular. I know this from my education."

"Then your education's wrong, I'm afraid. A planet like this, with a large moon..." Merlin left the sentence unfinished. "Spring tides and neap tides, Minla. No arguing with it."

"I'm sure you're right."

"Do you want the stone back?" he asked.

"Keep it, if it amuses you."

He closed his hand around the stone. "It still meant something to you when you gave it to me. It'll always mean something to me for that reason."

"Thank you for not leaving us. If my stone kept you here, it served a useful purpose."

"I'm glad I chose to stay. I just hope I haven't done more harm than good, with the things I showed you."

"That again," Minla said with a weary sigh. "You worry that we're going to blow ourselves to bits, just because you showed us the clockwork inside the atom."

"It's nasty clockwork."

He had seen enough progress, enough evidence of wisdom and independent ingenuity, to know that the Skyland forces would have a working atomic bomb within two years. By then, their rocket program would have given them a delivery system able to handle the cumbersome payload of that primitive device. Even if the rocket fell behind schedule, they only had to wait until the aerial landmass drifted over a Shadowland target.

"I can't stop you making weapons," Merlin said. "All I ask is that you use them wisely. Just enough to negotiate a victory, and then no more. Then forget about bombs and start thinking about atomic rockets."

Minla looked at him pityingly. "You worry that we're becoming monsters. Merlin, we already *were* monsters. You didn't make us any worse."

"That strain of bacterial meningitis was very infectious," Merlin said. "I know: I've run it through *Tyrant*'s medical analyzer. You were already having difficulties with supplies of antibiotics. If I hadn't landed, if I hadn't offered to make that medicine for you, your military effort might have collapsed within months. The Shadowlands would have won by default. There wouldn't be any need to introduce atomic bombs into the world."

"But we'd still need the rockets."

"Different technology. The one doesn't imply the other."

"Merlin, listen to me. I'm sorry that we're asking you to make these difficult moral choices. But for us it's about only one thing: species survival. If you hadn't dropped out of the sky, the Waynet would still be on its way to us, ready to slice our star in two. After that happened, you had no choice but to do everything possible to save us, no matter how bad a taste it leaves in your mouth."

"I have to live with myself when this is all over."

"You'll have nothing to be ashamed of. You've made all the right decisions so far. You've given us a future."

"I need to clear up a few things for you," Merlin said. "It isn't a friendly galaxy. The creatures that smashed your sky are still out there. Your ancestors forged the armored sky to hide from them, to make Lecythus look like an airless world. The Huskers were hunting down my own people before I left to work on my own. It isn't going to be plain sailing."

"Survival is better than death. Always and forever."

Merlin sighed: he knew that this conversation had run its course, that they had been over these things a thousand times already and were no closer to mutual understanding. "When I wake up again, I want to see lights in the sky."

"When I was a girl," Minla said, "long before you came, my father would tell me stories of people traveling through the void, looking down on Lecythus. He'd put in jokes and little rhymes, things to make me laugh. Under it all, though, he had a serious message. He'd show me the pictures in my books, of the great ship that brought us to Lecythus. He said we'd come from the stars and one day we'd find a way to go back there. It seemed like a fantasy when I was a little girl, something that would never come to pass in the real world. Yet now it's happening, just as my father always said it would. If I live long enough, I'll know what it's like to leave Lecythus behind. But I'll be dead long before we ever reach another world, or see any of the wonders you've known."

For an instant Minla was a girl again, not a driven military leader. Something in her face spoke to Merlin across the years, breeching the defenses he had carefully assembled.

"Let me show you something."

He took her into *Tyrant*'s rear compartment and revealed the matte-black cone of the syrinx, suspended in its cradle. At Merlin's invitation, Minla was allowed to stroke its mirror-smooth surface. She reached out her hand gingerly, as if expecting to touch something very hot or very cold. At the last instant her fingertips grazed the ancient artifact and then held the contact, daringly.

"It feels old," she said. "I can't say why."

"It does. I've often felt the same thing."

"Old and very heavy. Heavier than it has any right to be. And yet when I look at it, it's somehow not quite there, as if I'm looking at the space where it used to be."

"That's exactly how it looks to me."

Minla withdrew her touch. "What is it?"

"We call it a syrinx. It's not a weapon. It's more like a key or a passport."

"What does it do?"

"It lets my ship use the Waynet. In their time the Waymakers must have made billions of these things, enough to fuel the commerce of a million worlds. Imagine that, Minla: millions of stars bound by threads of accelerated spacetime, each thread strung with thousands of glittering ships rushing to and fro, drops of honey on a thread of silk, each ship moving so close to the speed of light that time itself slowed almost to stillness. You could dine on one world, ride your ship to the Waynet and then take supper on some other world, under the falling light of another sun. A thousand years might have passed while you were riding the flow, but that didn't matter. The Waymakers forged an empire where a thousand years was just a lazy afternoon, a time to put off plans for another day." Merlin looked sadly at Minla. "That was the idea, anyway."

"And now?"

"We breakfast in the ruins, barely remember the glory that was, and scavenge space for the handful of still-functioning syrinxes."

"Could you take it apart, find out how it works?"

"Only if I felt suicidal. The Waymakers protected their secrets very well."

"Then it is valuable."

"Incalculably so."

Minla stroked it again. "It feels dead."

"It just isn't active yet. When the Waynet comes closer, the syrinx will sense it. That's when we'll really know it's time to get out of here." Merlin forced a smile. "But by then we'll be well on our way."

"Now that you've shown me this secret, aren't you worried that we'll take it from you?"

MINLA'S FLOWERS

"The ship wouldn't let you. And what use it would it be to you anyway?"

"We could make our own ship, and use your syrinx to escape from here."

Merlin tried not to sound too condescending. "Any ship you built would smash itself to splinters as soon as it touched the Waynet, even with the syrinx to help it. And you wouldn't achieve much anyway. Ships that use the Waynet can't be very large."

"Why is that?"

Merlin shrugged. "They don't need to be. If it only takes a day or two of travel to get anywhere—remember what I said about clocks slowing down—then you don't need to haul all your provisions with you, even if you're crossing to the other side of the galaxy."

"But could a bigger ship enter the Waynet, if it had to?"

"The entry stresses wouldn't allow it. It's like riding the rapids." Merlin didn't wait to see if Minla was following him. "The syrinx creates a path that you can follow, a course where the river is easier. But you still need a small boat to squeeze around the obstacles."

"Then no one ever made larger ships, even during the time of the Waymakers?"

"Why would they have needed to?"

"That wasn't my question, Merlin."

"It was a long time ago. I don't have all the answers. And you shouldn't pin your hopes on the Waynet. It's the thing that's trying to kill you, not save you."

"But when you leave us...you'll ride the Waynet, won't you?"

Merlin nodded. "But I'll make damned sure I have a head start on the collision."

"I'm beginning to see how this must all look to you," Minla said. "This is the worst thing that's ever happened to us, the end of our history itself. To you it's just a stopover, an incidental adventure. I'm sure there were hundreds of worlds before us, and there'll be hundreds more. That's right, isn't it?"

Merlin bridled. "If I didn't care about you all, I'd have left twenty years ago."

"You very nearly did. I know how close you came. My father spoke of it many times, his joy when you changed your mind."

"I had a change of heart," Merlin said. "Everyone's allowed that. You played a part in it, Minla. If you hadn't told Malkoha to give me that gift..."

"Then I'm glad I did, if it meant so much." Minla looked away, something between sadness and fascination on her face. "Merlin, before you sleep. Do something for me."

"Yes?"

"Make me flowers again. From some world I'll never ever see. And tell me their story."

THE PLANETARY GOVERNMENT aircraft was a sleek silver flying wing with its own atomic reactor, feeding six engines buried in air-smoothed nacelles. Minla had already led Merlin down a spiral staircase, into an observation cupola set under the thickest part of the wing. Now she touched a brushed-steel panel, causing armored slats to whisk open in rapid sequence. Through the green-tinted blast-proof glass they had an uninterrupted view of the surface rolling by underneath.

The ocean carried no evidence of the war, but there was hardly any stretch of land that hadn't been touched in some fashion. Merlin saw the rubble-strewn remains of towns and cities, some with the hearts gouged out by kilometer-deep craters. He saw flooded harbors, beginning to be clawed back by the greedy fingers of the sea. He saw swathes of gray-brown land where nothing grew anymore, and where only dead, petrified forests testified to the earlier presence of living things. Atomic weapons had been used in their thousands, by both sides. The Skylanders had been first, though, which was why the weapons had a special name on Lecythus. Because of the shape of the mushroom cloud that accompanied each burst, they called them Minla's Flowers.

She pointed out the new cities that had been built since the ceasefire. They were depressing to behold: grids of utilitarian blocks, each skull-gray multistory building identical to the others. Spidery highways linked the settlements, but not once did Merlin see any evidence of traffic or commerce.

"We're not building for posterity," she said. "None of those buildings have to last more than fifty years, and most of them will be empty long before that. By the time they start crumbling, there'll be no one alive on Lecythus."

"You're surely not thinking of taking everyone with you," Merlin said

"Why not? It seemed unthinkable forty years ago. But so did atomic war, and the coming of a single world state. Anything's within our reach now. With social planning, we can organize matters such that the population shrinks to a tenth of its present size. No children will be allowed to be born in the last twenty years. And we'll begin moving people into the Space Dormitories long before that."

Merlin had seen the plans for the dormitories, along with the other elements of Minla's evacuation program. There was already a small space station in orbit around Lecythus, but it would be utterly dwarfed by the hundred dormitories. The plans called for huge air-filled spheres, each of which would swallow one hundred thousand evacuees, giving a total in-orbit human presence of ten million people. Yet even as the Space Dormitories were being populated, work would be underway on the thousand Exodus Arks that would actually carry the evacuees out of the system. The Arks would be built in orbit, using materials extracted and refined from the moon's crust. Merlin had already indicated to Minla's experts that they could expect to find a certain useful isotope of helium in the topsoil of the moon, an isotope that would enable the Arks to be powered by nuclear fusion engines of an ancient and well-tested design.

"Forced birth control, and mass evacuation," he said, grimacing. "That's going to take some tough policing. What if people don't go along with your program?"

"They'll go along," Minla said.

"Even if that meant shooting a few, to make a point?"

"Millions have already died, Merlin. If it takes a few more to guarantee the efficient execution of the evacuation program, I see that as a price worth paying."

"You can't push human society that hard. It snaps."

"There's no such thing as society," Minla told him.

Presently she had the pilot bring them below supersonic speed, and then down to a hovering standstill above what Merlin took to be an abandoned building, perched near the shore amid the remains of what must once have been a great ocean seaport. The flying wing lowered itself on ducted jets, blowing dust and debris in all directions until its landing gear kissed scorched earth and the engines quietened.

"We'll take a stroll outside," Minla said. "There's something I want you to see. Something that will convince you of our seriousness."

"I don't need convincing."

"I want you to see it nonetheless. Take this cloak." She handed him a surprisingly heavy garment.

"Lead impregnated?"

"Just a precaution. Radiation levels are actually very low in this sector."

MINLA'S FLOWERS

They disembarked via an escalator that had folded down from the flying wing's belly, accompanied by a detachment of guards. The armed men moved ahead, sweeping the ground with things that looked like metal brooms before ushering Minla and Merlin forward. They followed a winding path through scorched rubble and junk, taking care not to trip over the obstacles and broken ground. Calliope had set during their descent and a biting wind was now howling into land from the sea, setting his teeth on edge. From somewhere in the distance a siren rose and fell on a mournful cycle. Despite Minla's assurance concerning the radioactivity, Merlin swore he could already feel his skin tingling. Overhead, stars poked through the thinning layer of moonlit clouds.

When at last he looked up, he saw that the solitary building was in fact an enormous stone monument. It towered a hundred meters above the flying wing, stepped like a ziggurat and cut and engraved with awesome precision. Letters in Lecythus A marched in stentorian ranks across the highest vertical face. Beyond the monument, gray-black water lapped at the shattered remains of a promenade. The monument was presumably designed to weather storms, but it would only take one spring tide to submerge its lower flanks completely. Merlin wondered why Minla's people hadn't set it on higher ground.

"It's impressive."

"There are a hundred monuments like this on Lecythus," Minla told him, drawing her cloak tighter around herself. "We faced them with whetstone, would you believe it. It turns out to be very good for making monuments, especially when you don't want the letters to be worn away in a handful of centuries."

"You built a hundred of these?" Merlin asked.

"That's just the start. There'll be a thousand by the time we're finished. When we are gone, when all other traces of our culture have been erased from time, we hope that at least one of these monuments will remain. Shall I read you the inscription?"

Merlin had still learned nothing of the native writing, and he'd neglected to wear the lenses that would have allowed *Tyrant* to overlay a translation.

"You'd better."

"It says that once a great human society lived on Lecythus, in peace and harmony. Then came a message from the stars, a warning that our world was to be destroyed by the fire of the sun itself, or something even worse. So we made preparations to abandon the world that had been our home for so long, and to commence a journey into the outer darkness of interstellar space, looking for a new home in the stars. One day, thousands or tens of thousands after our departure, you, the people who read this message, may find us. For now you are welcome to make of this world what you will. But know that this planet was ours, and it remains ours, and that one day we shall make it our home again."

"I like the bit about 'peace and harmony.'"

"History is what we write, not what we remember. Why should we tarnish the memory of our planet by enshrining our less noble deeds?"

"Spoken like a true leader, Minla."

At that moment one of the guards raised his rifle and projected a line of tracer fire into the middle distance. Something hissed and scurried into the cover of debris.

"We should be leaving," Minla said. "Regressives come out at night, and some of them are armed."

"Regressives?"

"Dissident political elements. Suicide cultists who'd rather die on Lecythus than cooperate in the evacuation effort. They're our problem, Merlin, not yours."

MINLA'S FLOWERS

He'd heard stories about the regressives, but dismissed them as rumour until now. They were the survivors of the war, people who hadn't submitted eagerly to the iron rule of Minla's new Planetary Government. Details that didn't fit into the plan, and which therefore had to be brushed aside or suppressed or given a subhuman name. He pulled the cloak tighter, anxious not to spend a minute longer on the surface than necessary. But even as Minla turned and began walking back to the waiting aircraft—moonlight picked out the elegant sweep of its single great wing—something tugged at him, holding him to the spot.

"Minla," he called, a crack in his voice.

She stopped and turned around. "What is it, Merlin?"

"I've something for you." He reached under the cloak and fished out the gift she had given him as a girl, holding it before him. He'd had it with him for days, waiting for the moment he hoped would never come.

Impatiently, Minla retraced her steps. "I said we should be leaving. What is it you want to give me?"

He handed her the sliver of whetstone. "A little girl gave me this. I don't think I know that little girl any more."

Minla looked at the stone with a curl of disgust on her face. "That was forty years ago."

"Not to me. To me it was less than a year. I've seen a lot of changes since you gave me that gift."

"We all have to grow up sometime, Merlin." For a moment he thought she was going to hand him back the gift, or at least slip it into one of her own pockets. Instead, Minla let it drop to the ground. Merlin reached to pick it up, but it was too late. The stone fell into a dark crack between two shattered paving slabs; Merlin heard the chink as it bounced off something and fell even deeper.

"It's gone."

"It was just a silly stone," Minla said. "That's all. Now let's be on our way."

Merlin looked back at the lapping waters as he followed Minla to the moonlit flying wing. Something about the whetstone, something about tides of that sea, something about the moon itself, kept nagging at the back of his mind. There was a connection, trivial or otherwise, that he was missing.

He was sure it would come to him sooner or later.

MINLA WALKED WITH a stick, clicking its hard metal shaft against the echoing flooring of the station's observation deck. Illness or injury had disfigured her since their last meeting; she wore her graying hair in a lopsided parting, hanging down almost to the collar on her right side. Merlin could not say for certain what had happened to Minla, since she was careful to turn her face away from him whenever they spoke. But in the days since his revival he had already heard talk of assassination attempts, some of which had apparently come close to succeeding. Minla seemed more stooped and frail than he remembered, as if she had worked every hour of those twenty years.

She interrupted a light beam with her hand, opening the viewing shields. "Behold the Space Dormitories," she said, declaiming as if she had audience of thousands rather than a single man standing only a few meters away. "Rejoice, Merlin. You played a part in this."

Through the window, wheeling with the gentle rotation of the orbital station, the nearest dormitory loomed larger than Lecythus in the sky. The wrinkled gray sphere would soon reach operational pressure, its skin becoming taut. The final sun mirrors were being assembled in place, manipulated by mighty

MINLA'S FLOWERS

articulated robots. Cargo rockets were coming and going by the minute, while the first wave of evacuees had already taken up residence in the polar holding pens.

Twenty dormitories were ready now; the remaining eighty would come online within two years. Every day, hundreds of atomic rockets lifted from the surface of Lecythus, carrying evacuees—packed into their holds at the maximum possible human storage density, like a kind of three-dimensional jigsaw of flesh and blood—or cargo, in the form of air, water and prefabricated parts for the other habitats. Each rocket launch deposited more radioactivity into the atmosphere of the doomed world. It was now fatal to breathe that air for more than a few hours, but the slow poisoning of Lecythus was of no concern to the Planetary Government. The remaining surface-bound colonists, those who would occupy the other dormitories when they were ready, awaited transfer in pressurised bunkers, in conditions that were at least as spartan as anything they would have to endure in space. Merlin had offered the services of *Tyrant* to assist with the evacuation effort, but as efficient and fast as his ship was, it would have made only a token difference to the speed of the exercise.

That was not to say that there were not difficulties, or that the program was exactly on schedule. Merlin was gladdened by the progress he saw in some areas, disheartened in others. Before he slept, the locals had grilled him for help with their prototype atomic rockets, seemingly in expectation that Merlin would provide magic remedies for the failures that had dogged them so far. But Merlin could only help in a limited fashion. He knew the basic principles of building an atomic rocket, but little of the detailed knowledge needed to circumvent a particular problem. Minla's experts were frustrated, and then dismayed. He tried explaining to them that though an atomic rocket might be primitive compared to the engines in *Tyrant*, that didn't mean it was simple, or that its construction didn't involve many subtle principles. "I know how a sailing ship works," he said, trying to explain himself. "But that doesn't mean I could build one myself, or show a master boatbuilder how to improve his craft."

They wanted to know why he couldn't just give them the technology in *Tyrant* itself.

"My ship is capable of self-repair," he'd said. "But it isn't capable of making copies of itself. That's a deep principle, embodied in the logical architecture at a very profound level."

"Then run off a blueprint of your engines. Let us copy what we need from the plans," they said.

"That won't work. The components in *Tyrant* are manufactured to exacting tolerances, using materials your chemistry can't even explain, let alone reproduce."

"Then show us how to improve our manufacturing capability, until we can make what we need."

"We don't have time for that. *Tyrant* was manufactured by a culture that had had over ten thousand years of experience in spacefaring, not to mention knowledge of industrial processes and inventions dating back at least as far again. You can't cross that kind of gap in fifty years, no matter how hard you might want to."

"Then what are we supposed to do?"

"Keep trying," Merlin said. "Keep making mistakes, and learning from them. That's all any culture ever does."

That was exactly what they had done, across twenty painful years. The rockets worked now, after a fashion, but they'd arrived late and there was already a huge backlog of people and parts to be shifted into space. The dormitories should have been finished and occupied by now, with work already underway on the fleet of Exodus Arks. But the Arks had met obstacles as well. The lunar colonization program had run into unanticipated difficulties, requiring that the Arks be assembled from components made on Lecythus. The atomic rocket production lines were already running at maximum capacity without the burden of carrying even more tonnage into space.

"This is good," Merlin told Minla. "But you still need to step things up."

"We're aware of that," she answered testily. "Unfortunately, some of your information proved less than accurate."

Merlin blinked at her. "It did?"

"Our scientists made a prototype for the fusion drive, according to your plans. Given the limited testing they've been able to do, they say it works very well. It wouldn't be a technical problem to build all the engines we need for the Exodus Arks. So I'm told, at least."

"Then what's the problem?"

Her hand gripped the walking stick like a talon. "Fuel, Merlin. You told us we'd find helium 3 in the topsoil of our moon. Well, we didn't. Not enough to suit our needs, anyway."

"Then you mustn't have been looking properly."

"I assure you we looked, Merlin. You were mistaken. Now we'll have to find fuel from an alternative source, and redesign our fusion drive accordingly. We'll need your help, if we aren't to fall hopelessly behind schedule." Minla extended a withered hand toward the wheeling view. "To have come so far, to have reached this point, and then *failed*...that would be worse than having never tried at all, don't you think?"

Chastened, Merlin scratched at his chin. "I'll do what I can. Let me talk to the fusion engineers."

"I've scheduled a meeting. They're *very* anxious to talk to you." Minla paused. "There's something you should know, though. They've seen you make a mistake. They'll still be interested in what you have to say. But don't expect blind acceptance of your every word. They know you're human now."

"I never said I wasn't."

"You didn't, no. I'll give you credit for that. But for a little while some of us allowed ourselves to believe it."

Minla turned and walked away, the tap of her stick echoing into the distance.

AS SPACE WARS went, it was brief and relatively tame, certainly by comparison with the awesome battles delineated in the Cohort's pictorial history. The timeworn frescos on the swallowships commemorated engagements where entire solar systems were reduced to mere tactical details, hills or ditches in the terrain of a much larger strategic landscape, and where the participants—human and Husker both—were moving at significant fractions of the speed of light and employing relativistic weapons of world-shattering destructive potential. A single skirmish could eat up many centuries of planetary time, whole lifetimes from the point of view of a starship's crew. The war itself was a thing inseparably entwined with recorded history, a monstrous choking structure with its roots reaching into the loam of deep time, and whose end must be assumed (by all except Merlin, at least) to lie in the unimaginably remote future.

Here, the theatre of conflict was considerably less than half a light-second in diameter, encompassing only the immediate space around Lecythus, with its girdle of half-finished dormitories and Exodus Arks. The battle lasted barely a dozen hours, between first and last detonation. With the exception of Merlin's own late intervention, no weapons more potent that hydrogen bombs were deployed. Horrific, certainly, but possessed of a certain genteel precision compared to the weapons that had consumed Plenitude.

MINLA'S FLOWERS

It began with a surprise strike from the surface, using a wave of commandeered atomic rockets. It seemed that the Regressives had gained control of one of the rocket-assembly-and-launch complexes. The rockets had no warheads, but that didn't matter: kinetic energy, and the explosive force stored in their atomic engines, was still enough to inflict havoc on their targets. The weapons had been aimed with surprising accuracy. The first wave destroyed half of the unfinished dormitories, inflicting catastrophic damage on many of the others. By the time the second wave was rising, orbital defenses had sprung into action, but by then it was too late to intercept more than a handful of the missiles. Many of the atomic rockets were being piloted by suicide crews, steering their charges through Minla's hastily-erected countermeasure screens. By the third hour, the Planetary Government was beginning to retaliate against Regressive elements using atmospheric-entry interceptors, but while they could pick away at enemy fortifications on the ground, they couldn't penetrate the antimissile cordon around the launch complex itself. Rogue warheads chipped away at the edges of aerial landmasses, sending mountain-sized boulders crashing to the surface. Even as the battle raged, brutal tidals waves ravaged the already-frail coastal communities. As the hours ticked by, Minla's analysts maintained a grim toll on the total numbers of surface and orbital casualties. In the fifth and sixth hours, more dormitories fell to the assault. Stray fire accounted for even more losses. A temporary ceasefire in the seventh hour was only caused by the temporary occultation of the launch complex by a medium-sized aerial landmass. When the skies were clear again, the rockets rose up with renewed fury.

"They've hit all but one of the Exodus Arks," Minla said, when the battle was in its ninth hour. "We just had time to move the final ship out of range of the atomics. But if they find a way to increase their reach, by eliminating more payload mass..." She turned her face from his. "It'll all have been for nothing, Merlin. They'll have won, and the last sixty years may as well have not happened."

He felt preternaturally calm, knowing exactly what was coming. "What do you want me to do?"

"Intervene," Minla said. "Use whatever force is merited."

"I offered once. You said no."

"You changed your mind once. Now I change mine."

Merlin went to *Tyrant*. He ordered the ship to deliver a concentrated charm-torp salvo against the compromised rocket facility, bringing more energy to bear on that one tiny area of land than had been deployed in all the years of the atomic wars. There was no need for him to accompany his ship; like a well-trained dog, *Tyrant* was perfectly capable of carrying out his orders without direct supervision.

They watched the spectacle from orbit. When the electric-white fire erupted on the horizon of Lecythus, brightening that entire limb of the planet in the manner of a stuttering cold sunrise, Merlin felt Minla's hand tighten around his own. For all her frailty, for all that the years had taken from her, there remained astonishing steel in that grip.

"Thank you," she said. "You may just have saved us all."

IT HAD BEEN ten years.

Lecythus and its sun now lay many light-weeks to stern. The one remaining Exodus Ark had reached five percent of the speed of light. In sixty years—faster, if the engine could be improved—it would streak into another system, one that might offer the possibility of landfall. It flew alongside the gossamer line of the Waynet, using the tube as cover from Husker long-range sensors. The Exodus Ark carried only

MINLA'S FLOWERS

twelve hundred exiles, few of whom would live long enough to see another world.

The hospital was near the core of the ship, safely distant from the sleeting energies of interstellar radiation or the exotic emissions of the Waynet. Many of its patients were veterans of the Regressive War, victims of the viciously ingenious injuries wrought by the close conjunction of vacuum and heat, radiation and kinetic energy. Most of them would be dead by the time the fusion engine was silenced for cruise phase. For now they were being afforded the care appropriate to war heroes, even those who screamed bloodcurdling pleas for the painkilling mercy of euthanasia.

In a soundproofed private annex of that same complex, Minla also lay in the care of machines. This time the assassins had come closer than ever before, and they had very nearly achieved their objective. Yet she'd survived, and the prognosis for a complete recovery—so Merlin was informed—was deemed higher than seventy-five percent. More than could be said of Minla's aides, injured in the same attack, but they were at least receiving the best possible care in *Tyrant*'s frostwatch cabinets. The exercise was, Merlin knew, akin to knitting together human-shaped sculptures from a bloody stew of meat and splintered bone, and then hoping that those sculptures would retain some semblence of mind. Minla would have presented no challenge at all, but the Planetary Director had declined the offer of frostwatch care herself, preferring to give up her place to one of her underlings. Knowing that, Merlin allowed himself a momentary flicker of empathy.

He walked into the room, coughing to announce himself. "Hello, Minla."

She lay on her back, her head against the pillow, though she was not asleep. Slowly she turned to face Merlin as he approached. She looked very old, very tired, but she still found the energy to form a smile.

"It's so good of you to come. I was hoping, but...I didn't dare ask. I know how busy you've been with the engine upgrade study."

"I could hardly not pay you a visit. Even though I had a devil of a job persuading your staff to let me through."

"They're too protective of me. I know my own strength, Merlin. I'll get through this."

"I believe you would."

Minla's gaze settled on his hand. "Are those for me?"

He had a bouquet of alien flowers. They were of a peculiar dark hue, a shade that ought to have appeared black in the room's subdued gold lighting yet which was clearly and unmistakably purple, revealed by its own soft inner illumination. They had the look of a detail that had been hand-tinted in a black-and-white photograph, so that it appeared to float above the rest of the image.

"Of course," Merlin said. "I always bring flowers, don't I?"

"You always used to. Then you stopped."

"Perhaps it's time to start again."

He set them by her bedside, in the watered vase that was already waiting. They were not the only flowers in the room, but the purple ones seemed to suck the very color from the others.

"They're very beautiful," Minla said. "It's like I've never seen anything precisely that color before. It's as if there's a whole circuit in my brain that's never been activated until now."

"I chose them especially. They're famous for their beauty."

Minla lifted her head from the pillow, her eyes brightening with curiosity. "Now you'll have to tell me where they're from."

"It's a long story."

"That never stopped you before."

"A world called Lacertine. It's ten thousand light-years from here; many days of shiptime, even in the Waynet. I don't even know if it still exists."

MINLA'S FLOWERS

"Tell me about Lacertine," she said, pronouncing the name of the world with her usual scrupulousness.

"It's a very beautiful planet, orbiting a hot blue star. They say the planet must have been moved into its present orbit by the Waymakers, from another system entirely. The seas and skies are a shimmering electric blue. The forests are a dazzle of purple and violet and pink; colors that you've only ever seen when you close your eyes against the sun and see patterns behind your eyelids. White citadels rise above the tree line, towers linked by a filigree of delicate bridges."

"Then there are people on Lacertine?"

Merlin thought of the occupants, and nodded. "Adapted, of course. Everything that grows on Lacertine was bioengineered to tolerate the scalding light from the sun. They say if something can grow there, it can grow almost anywhere."

"Have you been there?"

He shook his head ruefully. "I've never been within a thousand light-years of the place."

"I'll never see it. Nor any of the other places you've told me about."

"There are places I'll never see. Even with the Waynet, I'm still just one human man, with one human life. Even the Waymakers didn't live long enough to glimpse more than a fraction of their empire."

"It must make you very sad."

"I take each day as it comes. I'd rather take good memories from one world, than fret about the thousand I'll never see."

"You're a wise man," Minla said. "We were lucky to get you."

Merlin smiled. He was silent for many moments, letting Minla enjoy the last calmness of mind she would ever know. "There's something I need to tell you," he said eventually.

She must have heard something in his tone of voice. "What, Merlin?"

"There's a good chance you're all going to die."

Her tone became sharp. "We don't need you to remind us of the risks."

"I'm talking about something that's going to happen sooner rather than later. The ruse of shadowing the Waynet didn't work. It was the best thing to do, but there was always a chance..." Merlin spread his hands in exaggerated apology, as if there had ever been something he could have done about it. "*Tyrant*'s detected a Husker attack swarm, six elements lying a light-month ahead of you. You don't have time to steer or slow down. They'd shadow every move you made, even if you tried to shake them off."

"You promised us..."

"I promised you nothing. I just gave you the best advice I could. If you hadn't shadowed the Waynet, they'd have found you even sooner."

"We aren't using the ramscoop design. You said we'd be safe if we stuck to fusion motors. The electromagnetic signature..."

"I said you'd be safer. There were never ironclad guarantees."

"You lied to us." Minla turned suddenly spiteful. "I never trusted you."

"I did all in my power to save you."

"Then why are you standing there looking so calm, when you know we're going to die?" But before Merlin had time to answer, Minla had seen the answer for herself. "Because you can leave," she said, nodding at her own percipience. "You have your ship, and a syrinx. You can slip into the Waynet and outrun the enemy."

"I'm leaving," Merlin said. "But I'm not running."

"Aren't they one and the same?"

"Not this time. I'm going back to Plenitude, I mean Lecythus, to do what I can for the people we left behind. The people you condemned to death."

MINLA'S FLOWERS

"Me, Merlin?"

"I examined the records of the Regressive War: not just the official documents, but *Tyrant*'s own data logs. And I saw what I should have seen at the time, but didn't. It was a ruse. It was too damned easy, the way they took control of that rocket factory. You let them, Minla."

"I did nothing of the kind."

"You knew the whole evacuation project was never going to be ready on time. The Space Dormitories were behind schedule, there were problems with the Exodus Arks…"

"Because you told us falsehoods about the helium in the moon's soil."

Merlin raised a warning hand. "We'll get to that. The point is, your plans were in tatters. But you could still have completed more dormitories and ships, if you'd been willing to leave the system a little later. You could still have saved more people than you did, albeit at a slightly increased risk to your own survival. But that wasn't acceptable. You wanted to leave there and then. So you engineered the whole Regressive attack, set it up as a pretext for an early departure."

"The Regressives were real!" Minla hissed.

"But you gave them the keys to that rocket silo, and the know-how to target and guide those missiles. Funny how their attack just missed the one station that you were occupying, you and all your political cronies, and that you managed to move the one Exodus Ark to safety just in time. Damned convenient, Minla."

"I'll have you shot for this, Merlin."

"Good luck. Try laying a hand on me, and see how far it gets you. My ship's listening in on this conversation. It can put proctors into this room in a matter of seconds."

"And the moon, Merlin? Do you have an excuse for the error that cost us so dearly?"

"I don't know. Possibly. That's why I'm going back to Lecythus. There are still people on the surface—Regressives, allies, I don't care. And people you abandoned in orbit as well."

"They'll all die. You said it yourself."

He raised a finger. "If they don't leave. But maybe there's way. Again, I should have seen it sooner. But that's me all the way. I take a long time to put the pieces together, but I get there in the end. Just like Dowitcher, the man who gave your father the whetstone."

"It was just a stone."

"So you said. In fact, it was a vital clue to the nature of your world. It took spring tides and neap tides to lay down those patterns. But you said it yourself: Lecythus doesn't have spring tides and neap tides. Not any more, at least."

"I'm sure this means something to you."

"Something happened to your moon, Minla. When that whetstone formed, your moon was raising tides on Lecythus. When the moon and Calliope were tugging on your seas in the same direction, you got a spring tide. When they were balancing each other, you got a neap tide. Hence the patterning on the whetstone. But now the tides are the same from day to day. Calliope's still there, so that only leaves the moon. It isn't exerting the same gravitational pull it used to. Oh, it weighs *something*—but the effect is much reduced, and if you could skip forward a few hundred million years and examine a piece of whetstone laid down now, you'd probably find very faint variations in sediment thickness. But whatever the effect is now, it must be insignificant compared to the time when your whetstone was formed. Yet the moon's still there, in what appears to be the same orbit. So what's happened?"

"You tell me, Merlin."

"I don't think it's a moon anymore. I think the original moon got ripped to pieces to make your armored sky. I don't know how much of the original mass got used for that, but I'm guessing it was quite a significant fraction. The question is, what happened to the remains?"

"I'm sure you have a theory."

"I think they made a fake moon out of the leftovers. It sits there in your sky, it orbits Lecythus, but it doesn't pull on your seas the way the old one used to. And because it's new—relatively speaking—it doesn't have the soil chemistry we'd expect of a real moon, one that's been sitting there for billions of years, drinking in solar winds. That's why you didn't find the helium you were expecting."

"So what is it?"

"That's what I'm keen to find out. The thing is, I know what Dowitcher was thinking now. He knew that wasn't a real moon. Which begs the question: what's inside it? And could it make a difference to the survivors you left behind?"

"Hiding inside a shell won't help them," Minla said. "You already told us we'd achieve nothing by digging tunnels into Lecythus."

"I'm not thinking about hiding. I'm thinking about moving. What if the moon's an escape vehicle? An Exodus Ark big enough to take the entire population?"

"You have no evidence."

"I have this." With that, Merlin produced one of Minla's old picture books. Seventy years had aged its papers to a brittle yellow, dimming the vibrancy of the old inks. But the linework in the illustrations was still clear enough. Merlin held the book open to a particular page, letting Minla look at it. "Your people had a memory of arriving on Lecythus in a moon-sized ship," he said. "Maybe that was true. Equally, maybe it was a case of muddling one thing with another. I'm wondering if the thing you were meant to remember was not that you came by moon, but that you could leave by one."

Minla stared at the picture. For a moment, like a breeze on a summer's day, Merlin felt a wave of almost unbearable sadness pass through the room. It was as if the picture had transported her back to her childhood, before she had set her life on the trajectory that, seventy years later, would bring it to this bed, this soundproofed room, the shameful survival of this one ship. The last time she had looked at the picture, everything had been possible, all life's opportunities open to her. She'd been the daughter of a powerful and respected man, with influence and wisdom at her fingertips. And yet from all the choices presented to her, she had selected this one dark path, and followed it to its conclusion.

"Even if it is a ship," she said softly, "you'll never get them all aboard."

"I'll die trying."

"And us? We get abandoned to our fates?"

Merlin smiled: he'd been expecting the question. "There are twelve hundred people on this ship, some of them children. They weren't all party to your schemes, so they don't all deserve to die when you meet the Huskers. That's why I'm leaving behind weapons and a detachment of proctors to show you how to install and use them."

For the first time since his arrival in the room, Minla spoke like a leader again. "Will they make a difference?"

"They'll give your ship a fighting chance. That's the best I can offer."

"Then we'll take what we're given."

"I'm sorry it came to this. I played a part in what you became, of that I've no doubt. But I didn't make you a monster."

"No," she said. "I'll at least take credit for myself, and for the fact that I saved twelve hundred of my people. If it took a monster to do that, doesn't that mean we sometimes need monsters?"

MINLA'S FLOWERS

"Maybe we do. But that doesn't mean we should forgive them for what they are, even for an instant." Gently, as if bestowing a gift, Merlin placed the picture book on Minla's recumbant form. "I'm afraid I have to go now. There won't be much time when I get back to Lecythus."

"Please," she said. "Not like this. Not this way."

"This is how it ends," he said, before turning from her bed and walking to the exit. "Goodbye, Minla."

Twenty minutes later he was in the Waynet, racing back to Lecythus.

THERE'S A LOT to tell, and one day I'll get around to writing it up properly. For now it's enough to say that I was right to trust my instincts about the moon. I just wish I'd put the clues together sooner than I did. Perhaps then Minla would never have had to commit her crimes.

I didn't save as many as I'd have wished, but I did save some of the people Minla left behind to die. I suppose that has to count for something. It was close, but if there's one thing to be said for Waymaker-level technology, it's that it's almost childishly easy to use. They were like babies with the toys of the gods. They left that moon there for a good reason, and while it was necessary for them to camouflage it—it had to be capable of fooling the Huskers, or whoever they built that sky to hide from—the moon itself was obligingly easy to break into, once our purpose became clear. And once it started moving, once its great engines came online after tens of thousands of years of quiet dormancy, no force in the universe could have held it back. I shadowed the fleeing moon long enough to establish that it was headed into a sector that appeared to be free of Husker activity, at least for now. It'll be touch-and-go for a few centuries, but with Force and Wisdom on their side, I think they'll make it.

I'm in the Waynet now, riding the flow away from Calliope. The syrinx still works, much to my relief. For a while I considered riding the contraflow, back toward that lone Exodus Ark. By the time I reached them they'd have been only days away from the encounter. But my presence wouldn't have made a decisive difference to their chances of surviving the Huskers, and I couldn't have expected much of a warm welcome.

Not after my final gift to Minla.

I'm glad she never asked me too much about those flowers, or the world they came from. If she'd wanted to know more about Lacertine, she might have sensed that I was holding something back. Such as the fact that the assassin guilds on Lacertine were masters of their craft, known throughout the worlds of the Waynet for their skill and cunning, and that no guild on Lacertine was more revered than the bioartificers who made the sleepflowers.

It was said that they could make them in any shape, any color, to match any known flower from any known world. It was said that they could pass all tests save the most microscopic scrutiny. It was said that if you wanted to kill someone, you gave them a gift of flowers from Lacertine.

She would have been dead not long after my departure. The flowers would have detected her presence—they were keyed to locate a single breathing form in a room, most commonly a sleeper—and when the room was quiet they would have become stealthily animate, leaving their jar and creeping from point to point with the slowness of a sundial's shadow, their movement imperceptible to the naked eye, but enough to take them to the face of the sleeper. Their tendrils would have closed around Minla's face with the softness of a lover's caress. Then the paralyzing toxins would have hit her nervous system.

I hoped it was painless. I hoped it was quick. But what I remembered of the Lacertine assassins was that they were known for their cleverness, not their clemency.

MINLA'S FLOWERS

Afterward, I deleted the sleepflowers from the biolibrary.

I knew Minla for less than a year of my life, and for seventy years by another reckoning. Sometimes when I think of her I see a human being in all her dimensions, as real as anyone I've ever known. Other times, I see something two-dimensional, like a faded illustration in one of her books, so thin that the light shines through her.

I don't hate her, even now. But I wish time and tide had never brought us together.

A comfortable number of light-hours behind me, the Waynet has just cut into Calliope's heart. It has already sliced through the photosphere and the star's convection zone. Quite what has happened, or is happening, or will happen, when it touched (or touches, or will touch) the nuclear-burning core is still far from clear.

Theory says that no impulse can travel faster than light. Since my ship is already riding the Waynet's flow at very nearly the speed of light, it seems impossible that any information concerning Calliope's fate will ever be able to catch up with me. And yet...several minutes ago I swear that I felt a kick, a jolt in the smooth glide of my flight, as if some report of that destructive event had raced up the flow at superluminal speed, buffeting my little ship.

There's nothing in the data to suggest any unusual event, and I don't have any plans to return to Lecythus and see what became of that world when its sun was gored open. But I still felt something, and if it reached me up the flow of the Waynet, if that impulse by-passed the iron barrier of causality itself, I can't begin to imagine the energies that must have been involved, or what must have happened to the strand of the Waynet behind me. Perhaps it's unraveling, and I'm about to breathe my last breath before I become a thin smear of naked quarks, stretched across several billion kilometers of interstellar space.

That would certainly be one way to go.

Frankly, it would be nice to have the luxury to dwell on such fears. But I still have a gun to find, and I'm not getting any younger.

Mission resumed.

"It'll have to be," I said.

"Something worries me, though," Purslane said. "We still haven't told anyone that my strand wasn't all it appears to be. They'll have to find out one of these days."

"Not tonight, though."

"Campion…if my name comes out of the hat…*what will I do?*"

I feigned concern, suppressing an amused smile. "Do what I'd do. Keep a very straight face."

"You mean…just accept it? That would be a little on the mischievous side, wouldn't it?"

"Very," I said. "But worth it, all the same."

Purslane tightened her grasp on my arm. Together we walked back toward the auditorium where the others waited. Under us, the fires of creation consumed my little world while, far above it, aquatics gathered in squadrons and schools, ready for their long migration.

"What?"

"I shouldn't even mention it…but I've been less than discrete about my flight plan. That trick I used to break into Burdock's ship? It worked equally well with yours."

"What did you do?"

"Nothing harmful. Just installed a copy of my flight plan on your ship…for your information. Just so you know where I am."

"You're right," I said, wonderingly. "That was spectacularly indiscrete."

"I couldn't help it."

"It would be completely improper for us to meet."

"Utterly," Purslane agreed, nodding emphatically.

"But you'll stick to that flight plan?"

"To the letter." She had finished her wine. She flung the empty glass into space. I watched it fall, waiting for the glint when it impacted the bubble. But before it hit, Purslane took my arm and turned me away from the view. "Come on, Campion. Let's go inside. They're still all waiting to hear who's won best strand."

"I can't believe anyone still cares about that, after all that's happened."

"Never underestimate the recuperative powers of human vanity," Purslane said sagely. "Besides: it isn't just the strand we have to think about. There are two memorials that need to be created. We'll need one for Burdock, and one for Fescue."

"One day we might need one for Samphire as well," I said.

"I think we'll do our best to forget all about him."

"He won't go away that easily. He may still be alive. Or it may be that he was murdered and replaced with an impostor, just like Burdock. Either way, I have a feeling we haven't finished with him. Or the Great Work."

"We've won this battle, though. That's enough for tonight, isn't it?"

"It's probably gone now," I said sadly. "They don't last long, compared to us."

"But perhaps you'll find an even better one."

"I'll keep my eyes open. I mapped some promising rivers during my tour; places where the geology might have allowed waterfalls to form by now. I think I'll revisit some of those old places, for old time's sake."

"Bring me back a memory."

"I'll be sure to. It's just such a shame you won't ever see them with your own eyes…" I paused, aware that I stood on the thrilling, dangerous threshold of something. "I mean with me, the two of us."

"You know the line frowns upon planned associations," Purslane said, as if I needed to be reminded. "Such meetings erode the very spirit of chance and adventure Abigail sought to instill in us. If we meet between now and the next reunion, it must be by chance and chance alone."

"Then we'll never meet."

"No. Probably not."

"That's a silly rule, isn't it? I mean, given everything else that's happened here…why should we care?"

Purslane was a great while answering. "Because we're traditionalists, Campion. Line loyalists, to the marrow." She tightened her grip on the rail as something came streaking up from the molten world below: the last of my aquatics, lingering out of idleness or some instinctive curiosity. The huge field-encased creature was as sleek as night, its under parts highlit in brassy reds from the fires. It paused at the level of the balcony, long enough to scrutinise us with one small, wrinkled, distressingly human eye. Then with a powerful flick of its fluke it soared higher, to the orbital shallows where its fellow were already assembling.

"There is something, though," Purslane added.

"I couldn't very well let them stay in the ocean."

"It was lovely. Putting aside everyone else that happened...I think that was my favourite bit. Not that this is bad, either."

We paused a while to watch a succession of major impacts: a long, sequenced string of them. Continent-sized fissures were beginning to open up deep into the planet's mantle: wounds as bright as day.

"I created something and now I'm ruining it. Doesn't that strike you as just the tiniest bit...infantile? Fescue certainly wouldn't have approved."

"I don't know," she said. "It's not as if that world ever had any chance of outlasting us. It was created to endure for a specific moment in time. Like a sandcastle, or an ice sculpture. Here, and then gone. In a way, that's the beauty of it. Who'd marvel at a sandcastle, if sandcastles lasted forever?"

"Or sunsets, I suppose," I said.

"Oh, no," she said. "Don't start talking about sunsets again. I thought you got that safely out of your system last time."

"I have," I said. "Completely and utterly. I'm thinking of a radically different theme for my tour this time. Something as far removed from sunsets as possible."

"Oh, good."

"Something like...waterfalls."

"Waterfalls."

"They're pretty universal, you know. Any planet with some kind of atmosphere, and some kind of surface, usually ends up with something vaguely like a waterfall, somewhere. As long as you're not too fussy about the water part."

"Actually," Purslane said, "I quite like waterfalls. I remember one I encountered in my travels...ten vertical kilometers of it, pure methane. I stood under it, allowed myself to feel a little of the cold. Just enough to shiver at the wonder of it."

She touched a finger to her lips. "I know. Isn't that enough for you?"

○←

A LITTLE LATER, Purslane and I stood alone on the highest balcony of the island's central spire. The island had climbed out of what would have been Reunion's atmosphere, had the atmosphere remained.

Far below, viewed through the flickering curtain of the containment bubble, my planet writhed in the agonies of its death by stoning. The impacting asteroids struck her like fists, bludgeoning her in furious quick-time. At least two, sometimes three or four, arrived within every minute. Their impact fireballs had dispersed most of the atmosphere by now, and had elevated a goodly fraction of the crust into parabolas of molten rock, tongues of flame that arced thousands of kilometers before splashing down. They reminded me of the coronal arcs near the surface of a late-type star. The ocean was a memory: boiled into a dust-choked vapour. Concussion from the multiple impacts was already unhinging the delicate clockwork of the planet's magnetohydrodynamic core. Had there been a spot on the planet where it was still night, the auroral storms would have been glorious. For a moment, I regretted that I had not arranged matters so that the aurorae had formed part of the show, somehow, someway.

But it was much too late for second thoughts now. It would be someone else's turn next time.

Purslane took my hand. "Don't look so sad, Campion. You did well. It was a fine end."

"You think so?"

"They'll be raving about this for a million years. What you did with those whales..." She shook her head in undisguised admiration.

"He believed it would be for the best. But more than likely he was sounding you out, seeing what you thought of it, goading you into an indiscretion." Vetchling looked to the simmering sea, punctured by hundreds of volcanic vents that had reopened in the planet's crust. We were looking down on the sea from a dizzy height now: the island had detached itself from Reunion, and was now climbing slowly into space, pushed by the vast motors I must have installed in its foundation rocks. The blast from Samphire's weapon had shattered the outlying islands, crumbling them back into the sea. The water had rushed into the fill the caldera left after the main island's departure, and now there was no trace that it had ever existed.

The party was over.

"He suspected Advocate involvement in the crime," Vetchling continued. "But he could not rule out someone else being implicated: a sleeper, an agent no one would suspect."

"He must have suspected Purslane and I," I said.

"That's possible. You did spend a lot of time associating, after all. If it's any consolation, the two of you wouldn't have been his only suspects. He may even have had his suspicions about Samphire."

"What will happen to the Great Work now?"

"That's not just a matter for Gentian Line," Vetchling said. "But my guess is there'll be pressure to put the whole thing on the back burner for a few hundred thousand years. A cooling-off period." She sounded sad. "Fescue was respected. He had a lot of friends beyond our line."

"I hated him," I said.

"He wouldn't have minded. All he really cared about was the line. You did the right thing, Campion."

"I killed him."

"You saved us all. You have Fescue's gratitude."

"How can you know?" I asked.

not been flung so far out in space. It had been an accidental whim of design, but it had saved us all.

So had Fescue.

THERE WAS A great space battle that night, but this time it was for real, not staged in memory of some ancient, time-fogged conflict. The real Samphire had been on his ship, and when the construct failed to destroy the island, he made a run for orbit. From orbit, he must have planned to turn the ship's own armaments on Reunion. But Fescue's allies had anticipated him, and when his ship moved, so did a dozen others. They made interception above the lacerated atmosphere of my dying world and lit the sky with obscene energies. Samphire died, or at least that version of Samphire that had been sent to infiltrate our gathering. It may or may not have been the final one. It may or may not have been the only impostor in our midst.

After the battle, Vetchling, one of the other Advocates, took me aside and told me what she knew.

"Fescue supported the Great Work," she said. "But not at any cost. When evidence reached him that an atrocity had been committed in the name of the Work…the murder of an entire human culture…he realised that not all of us shared his view."

"Then Fescue knew all along," I said, dismayed.

"No. He had shards of intelligence—hints, rumours, whisperings. He still had no idea who had committed the crime; how deeply they were tied to Gentian Line. He did not know whether the rest of the Advocates could be trusted." She paused. "He trusted me, and a handful of others. But not everyone."

"But Fescue spoke to me about the Great Work," I said. "Of how we all had to bind together to bring it into being."

They were standing only a few meters apart. It would only cost me a moment's concentration to order that part of the floor to detach itself, falling free. But if I did that, I would be sending Fescue to his death.

"Do it!" he hissed.

"I can't," I said.

"Campion," he said. "I know you and I have had our differences. I have always criticised you for lacking spine. Well, now is your chance to prove me wrong. *Do this*."

"I…"

"Do it! For the sake of the line!"

I looked at the faces of the other line members. I saw their pain, but also their solemn consent. They were telling me I had no choice. They were telling me to kill Fescue, and save us all.

I did it.

I willed the floor around the two figures to detach itself from the rest of the balcony. The tiny machines forming the fabric of the floor followed my will with dumb obedience, severing the molecular bonds that linked each machine to its neighbour.

For a heart-rending moment, the floor seemed to hover in place.

The field around Samphire quivered, beginning to lose integrity. Fescue's generators were running out of power, Fescue running out of concentration…

He looked at me and nodded. "Good work, Campion."

Then they dropped.

It was a long way down, and they were still falling when the revellers surged to the edge of the balcony to look down. The light from the explosion momentarily eclipsed the brightest impacts still raining down on the planet. I nodded at Fescue's assessment: kilotonne range, easily. He had been right. It would have killed us all, and snapped the spire in two had the balcony like two theatrical curtains, showing no pain. Instead of muscle and bone, we saw only an oozing clockwork of translucent pink machines, layered around a glowing blue core.

"Homunculus machinery," Fescue said, with an awesome calm. "He's a weapon."

Samphire smiled. A white light curdled in his open chest. It brightened to hellfire, ramming from his mouth and eyes. The construct body writhed as the detonating weapon consumed its nervous system from within. The outer layers crisped and collapsed.

But something was containing the blast. The white light—almost too bright to look at now—could not escape. It was being held back by a man-sized containment bubble, locked around Samphire.

I looked at Fescue. He stood with his arms outstretched, like a sculptor visualising a composition. Thick metal jewellery glinted on his fingers. Not jewellery, I realised now, but miniature field generators. Fescue was holding the containment bubble around Samphire, preventing the blast from escaping and destroying us all. His face was etched with the strain of controlling the generators.

"I'm not sure of the yield," Fescue said to me, forcing each word out. "Sub-kilotonne range, I think, or else your systems would have detected the homunculus machinery. But it will still be enough to destroy this balcony. Can the island lock a screen around him?"

"No," I said. "I never allowed for…this."

"That's as I thought. I can't hold it much longer…twenty-five, thirty seconds." Fescue's eyes bored into me with iron determination. "You have complete control of the structure, Campion? You can reshape it according to your requirements?"

"Yes," I said, faltering.

"Then you must drop the two of us through the floor."

You've always had an interest in ancient weapons, Samphire... especially the weapons of the Homunculus wars."

Samphire looked astonished. "That was over a million years ago. It's ancient history!"

"But what's a million years to the Gentian Line? You knew where those weapons were to be found, and you probably had more than an inkling of how they worked."

"No," Samphire said. "This is preposterous."

"It may well be," Fescue allowed. "In which case, you'll be allowed all the time you need to make your case, before a jury of your peers. If you are innocent, we'll prove it and ask your forgiveness—just as we did with Betony, all those years ago. If you are guilty, we will prove that instead—and uncover the rest of your collaborators. You've never struck me as the calculating kind, Samphire: I doubt that you put this together without assistance."

A wave of change overcame Samphire: his expression hardening. "You can prove what you like," he said. "It will change nothing."

"That sounds suspiciously like an admission of guilt," Fescue said. "Is it true? Did you really murder an entire culture, just to protect the Great Work?"

Now his expression was full of disdain. There was an authority in his voice I had never heard before. "One culture," Samphire said. "One pebble on the beach, against an ocean of possibility! Do you honestly think they mattered? Do you honestly think we'll remember them, in a billion years?"

Fescue turned to his Advocate friends. "Restrain him."

Three of the Advocates took purposeful steps toward Samphire. But they had only taken three or four paces when Samphire shook his head, more in sorrow than anger, and ripped open his tunic, exposing his smooth and hairless chest to the waist. He plunged his fingers into his own skin and pulled it aside bright frothing wound into the sea. Sensing danger, the island's screen came on, muting the impact blast to a salty roar. Another trail lanced down fifty kilometers away, raising a huge plume of superheated steam.

The impacts were increasing in severity.

Fescue spoke again. "We've all seen the evidence Purslane submitted. Given the truth about Burdock…I believe we should take the rest of the story seriously. Including the part about the murder of an entire culture." He looked at the two of us. "You wanted to see our anticollision fields, I believe."

"That'll tell us who did it," Purslane said.

"I think you may shortly have your wish."

He was right. All around the island, the ships were raising their screens again, as protection against the bombardment. The smaller ships at first, then the larger ones—all the way up to the biggest craft of all, those that were already poking into space. The screens quivered and stabilised, and a hail of minor impacts glittered off them.

"Well," Fescue said, addressing Purslane. "Do you see a match?"

"Yes," she said. "I do."

Fescue nodded grimly. "Would you care to tell us who it is?"

Purslane blinked, paralysed by the enormity of what she had to reveal. I held her hand, willing her to find the strength. "I thought it might be you," she told Fescue. "Your ship matched the size profile…and when you ruined Campion's ploy…"

"I don't think he meant to," I said.

"No, he didn't," Purslane said. "That's obvious now. And in any case, his ship isn't the best match. Samphire's ship, on the other hand…"

As one, the crowd's attention locked onto Samphire. "No," he said. "There's been a mistake."

"Perhaps," Fescue said. "But there is the matter of the weapons Purslane mentioned: the ones used against Grisha's people.

signalled some terrible impact. Something large had smashed into my world. As more trails of light split the sky, I sensed that it would not be the last.

The island shook beneath our feet. That made no sense at all: there surely hadn't been enough time for shockwaves to reach us yet, but none of us had imagined the vibration. I steadied myself on the handrail.

"What..." Purslane began.

The island shook again. That was a cue for the crowd to renew their interest in me, tearing their attention away from the departing aquatics. Purslane squeezed closer to me. I tightened my hold on her, while she redoubled her hold on me.

The crowd advanced.

"Stop," boomed out a voice.

Everyone halted and turned to look at the speaker. It was Fescue, and he was kneeling by the figure I had shot. He had a hand in the wound I had bored through the body, plunged deep to the wrist. Slowly he withdrew his hand, slick to the cuff with blood, but holding something between his fingers, something that wriggled in them like a little silver starfish.

"This wasn't Burdock," he said, standing to his feet, while still holding the obscene, wriggling thing. "It was...a thing. Just like Campion and Purslane told us." Fescue turned to look at me, his expression grave and forgiving. "You told the truth."

"Yes," I said, with all the breath I could muster. I realised that I had been wrong about Fescue: utterly, utterly wrong.

"Then it's true," he said. "One of us has committed a crime."

"Burdock's body is still on his ship," I said. "All of this can be proved...if you allow us."

The ground shook again. Overhead, the meteor assault had become continuous, and the horizon was aglow with fire. I had no sooner registered this than a small shard slammed out of the sky no more than fifteen kilometers from the island, punching a

"To where?"

"You tell me, Campion."

But I didn't have to tell her. It was soon obvious. In ones and twos they started leaving the ocean, rising into the air. Curtains of water drained off their flanks as they parted company with the sea. Ones and twos at first, then whole schools of them, rising into the sky between the hovering cliffs of our ships, as if they were born to fly.

"This is…impossible," I said. "They're aquatics. They don't… fly."

"Unless you made them that way. Unless you always planned this."

Pink-tinged aurorae flickered around the rising forms, hinting at the fields that allowed them to fly, and which would—I presumed—sustain them when the air thinned out, high above us. Some ghost of a memory now pushed its way into my consciousness. Had I truly engineered these aquatics for flight, equipping them with implanted field generators, and enough animal wisdom to use them? The memory beckoned, and then shrivelled under my attention.

"Maybe," I said.

"Good," Purslane said. "But now the next question: why?"

But we didn't have long to wonder about that. Suddenly the sky was cut in two by a brighter meteor than any we had seen during the earlier display. It boomed, reverberating down to the horizon and left a greenish aftertinge.

Another followed it: brighter now.

As if the meteor had triggered something, the sea erupted with a vast wave of departing aquatics. Thousands of them now, packed into huge and ponderous shoals or flocks, each aggregation moving with its own dim identity. The seas were emptying of life. Another meteor slashed the sky, bringing a temporary daylight to the scene. Over the horizon, an ominous false dawn away. I received a desultory kick, and then they left me there, sprawled on the ground, my mouth wet, my body bruised. I knew they hadn't finished with me. They were just leaving me alone while something else attracted their attention.

In their hundreds, they were pressing against the low railing that encircled the balcony. They were looking out to sea, drawn by something going on beyond the island. I pushed myself to my feet and stumbled to the slumped form of Purslane. They had not hurt her as badly as me, but there was still a cut on her lip where someone had slapped her.

"Are you all right?" I said, my mouth thick with blood.

"Better than you," she said.

"I don't think they're done with us. There's a distraction now…maybe we could reach our ships?"

She shook her head and used her finger to wipe blood from my chin. "We started this, Campion. Let's finish it."

"It's Fescue," I said. "He's the one."

We followed the onlookers to the balcony. No one gave us a second glance, even as we pushed forward to the front. All round us the revellers were looking at the sea. Sleek dark forms were surfacing from the midnight waters, black as night themselves. They lolled and bellied in the waves, pushing great flukes and flippers into the sky, jetting white spouts of water from blowholes.

Purslane asked me what was happening.

"I don't know," I said truthfully.

"You planned this, Campion. This has to be something to do with Thousandth Night."

"I know." I winced at the pain in my chest, certain that the mob had broken a rib. "But I don't remember what I planned. I thought the meteor shower was an end to it."

They were everywhere now, surfacing in multitudes. "It's as if they're gathering in readiness for something," Purslane said. "Like the start of a migration."

and they wanted him dead, with someone else to pin the blame on? Suddenly I felt dizzy, lost in mazelike permutations of bluff and double bluff. I had to make a simple choice. I had to trust my intuitive sense of what was true and what was false.

"If this is a mistake," I said, "forgive me."

I squeezed the trigger. The particle beam sliced its way across space, piercing the figure in the chest.

Burdock's impostor touched a hand to the smoking wound, opened its mouth as it speak, and fell lifeless to the floor. The crowd screamed their horror, revolted at the idea that a member of the Gentian Line had murdered another.

My work done, I let go of the particle gun. It remained floating before me, as if inviting me to take another shot. Burdock's impostor lay on its side, with one dry hand open to the sky. He had touched the wound and there had been no blood. I allowed myself a moment of relief. The others would see that the thing I had killed was not a man, but a bloodless construct. But even as these thoughts formed, the body retched and coughed a mouthful of dark blood onto the perfect white marble of the terrace. Its face was a mask of fear and incomprehension. Then it was still.

The crowd surged. They were on me in seconds, swatting aside the gun. They pulled me from the plinth and smothered me to the ground. The breath was knocked out of me. They began to pull at my clothing with animal fury. I heard shouts as some of the revellers tried to pull the others off me, but the collective anger—the collective repulsion—was too great to be resisted. I felt something crack in my chest, tasted my own blood as someone smashed a fist into my jaw. I thrashed out, survival instincts kicking in, but there were too many of them. Most of them were still wearing carnival masks.

Then something happened. Just before I was about to go under, the attack calmed. Someone landed a final punch in my chest, sending a bolt of pain up my spine, and then pulled

Fescue looked regretful. "Authentication can always be faked, with sufficient ingenuity. You've already admitted that you broke into his ship, after all. Disavow your involvement in this, Purslane, before it's too late."

"No," she said. "I won't."

Fescue nodded at a number of the people around him, including a handful of senior Advocates.

"Restrain the two of them," he said.

I fingered the metal shape under my flame-colored costume. My hand closed on the haft and removed Grisha's particle gun. The crowd silenced as the evil little thing glinted in the lantern light. Earlier, unwitnessed, I had primed the weapon onto Burdock. I squeezed a jewelled button and the gun moved as if in an invisible grip, nearly dragging itself from my fist. It swivelled onto Burdock and locked steady as a snake. Even if I released my hold on the gun, it would keep tracking its designated target.

"Stand aside, please," I said.

"Don't do anything silly," Fescue said, even as the crowd parted around Burdock's impostor.

The moment closed around me like a vice. I had seen the real, dying Burdock aboard his ship—at least, I believed I had. When I squeezed the trigger, I would be killing a mindless automaton, a biomechanical construct programmed to duplicate Burdock's responses with a high degree of accuracy...but not a living thing. Nothing with a sense of self.

But what if the dying figure on the ship was the impostor, and this was still the real Burdock? What if the whole story about Grisha and the assassination agent had been the lie, and the real Burdock was standing in front of me? I had no idea why such an elaborate charade might have been staged...but I couldn't rule it out, either. And there was one possibility that sprang to mind. What if Burdock had enemies among the line, the truth. Burdock was murdered by proponents of the Great Work, because Burdock knew what they had done."

Fescue looked intrigued. "Which was?"

"They destroyed an entire culture…Grisha's people…a culture that had uncovered Prior data damaging to the Great Work. Wiped them out with Homunculus weapons. Burdock tried to cover up his discovery, for fear of what the Advocates would do to him. There was a discrepancy in Burdock's dreams…an error." Purslane's control began to falter. "He said he'd been somewhere he hadn't…somewhere Campion had been."

"So it was Burdock's word against Campion?" Fescue turned to the impostor. "Does this make the slightest sense to you?"

The impostor shrugged and looked at me with something between pity and spite.

"Hear us out," Purslane insisted. "All Campion was hoping to do was provoke the raising of anticollision shields. The ship that destroyed Grisha's people…we had data on its field resonance, but we needed to see our own fields before we could establish a match." Purslane swallowed and regained some measure of calm. "I'm broadcasting the resonance data to all ships. See it for yourselves. See what those bastards did to Grisha's people."

There was a moment, a lull, while the crowd assessed the data Purslane had just made public. She had taken a frightful risk in revealing the information, for now our enemies had every incentive to move against us, even if that meant killing everyone else on the island. But I agreed with what she had done. We were out of options.

Except one.

"Very impressive," Fescue admitted. "But we've no evidence that you didn't forge this data."

"The authentication stamp ties it to Burdock," Purslane said.

twenty seconds, frozen in the gaze of nearly a thousand mortified onlookers. Then my thoughts suddenly quietened, as if I'd found an epicentre of mental calm. I seemed to stand outside myself.

"There is no winner," I said softly. "Not yet."

"Perhaps you ought to stand down," Fescue said. "You've arranged a fine reunion; we all agree on that. It would be a shame to ruin it now."

Fescue took a step toward me, presumably intending to help me from the plinth.

"Wait," I said, with all the dignity I could muster. "Wait and hear me out. All of you."

"You have an explanation for this travesty?" Fescue asked.

"Yes," I said. "I do."

He stopped in his tracks and folded his arms. "Then let's hear it. Part of me would love to think that this is all part of your Thousandth Night plans, Campion."

"Something awful has happened," I said. "There has been a conspiracy...a murder. One of us has been killed."

Fescue cocked his head. "One of us?"

I scanned the crowd and pointed to Burdock's duplicate. "That's not Burdock," I said. "That's an impostor. The real Burdock is dead."

The duplicate Burdock pulled a startled face. He looked at the people surrounding him, and then back at me, aghast. He said something and the onlookers laughed.

"The real Burdock is dead?" Fescue asked. "Are you quite sure of this, Campion?"

"Yes. I know because I've seen his body. When we broke into his ship..."

"When 'we' broke into his ship," Fescue repeated, silencing me. "You mean there was someone else involved?"

Purslane's voice rang out clear and true. "It was me. Campion and I broke into the ship. Everything he's told you is

My answer caught in my throat. "My ship may blow at any moment. Are you sure that secondary screen is going to be good enough?"

"Yes," Fescue said, with withering authority. "I'm more than sure."

The gathered revellers looked out to my ship, which remained stubbornly intact within the envelope Fescue had projected around it.

"Lower the island screen, Campion." And even as he spoke, Fescue's ship pushed mine up and away, into the high atmosphere, until it was lost among the stars.

The meteor shower was over, I noticed.

"The screen," Fescue said.

I gave the necessary commands, lowering the screen. "Thank you," I said, breathless and distraught. "That was… quick thinking, Fescue."

"It must have been a false alarm after all," he said, his unmasked eyes piercing mine. "Or a mistake."

"I thought my ship was going to blow up."

"Of course you did. Why else would you have told us?" He made a growl-like sound. "You were about to announce the winner, Campion. Perhaps you ought to continue."

There was a murmur of approval. If I'd had the sympathy of the crowd five minutes ago, I had lost it completely now. My throat was dry. I saw Purslane, the fox mask tugged down, and something like horror on her face.

"Campion," Fescue pushed. "The winner…if it isn't too much trouble."

But I didn't know the winner. The system wasn't due to inform me for another hour. I had delayed my receipt of the announcement, not wishing to be distracted from the main business.

"I….the winner. Yes. The winner of the strand…the best strand winner…is…the winner. And the winner is…" I fell silent for ten or

I said, tightening my face to a grimace. "I don't seem to be able to get a command through." I raised my voice, until I was almost shouting. "We're safe here: in a few seconds, I'll screen the island. Before I do that, I recommend that you order your ships to protect themselves."

Some of them already had. Their ships trembled within the vague, wobbling shapes of anticollision screens, like insects in spit. After a few seconds, the screens locked into stable forms and became harder to see. I allowed myself a glance in Purslane's direction. She responded with the tiniest encouraging nod.

It was working.

"Please," I urged. "Hurry. I'll raise the island's own screen in ten seconds. You may not be able to get a message through once that happens."

More and more ships wobbled as their screens flicked on. Peals of thunder, distant and low, signalled the activations. Doubtless many of the people were wondering what was going on: how it just happened that it was my ship that was threatening to blow up, when I was already the centre of attention. I just hoped that they would have the sense to put up their screens first and worry about the coincidence later.

But some of the largest ships were still not screened. I could not delay the screening of the island any longer. I would just have to hope that the necessary commands had already been sent, and that those ships were just a bit slow to respond.

But even as the island's own screen flickered on—blurring the view all around us, as if smeared glass had dropped into place—I knew that my plan was coming adrift.

Fescue spoke, his deep voice commanding instant attention. "The danger is passed," he said. "My own ship has projected a secondary screen around yours, Campion. You may lower the island's shield."

Mullein laughed good-naturedly, and, for a moment, he was the star of the show again. The gentle mocking of one of our number was also part of tradition. Of all us, Mullein could relax now.

"In a little while, we will return to our ships," I continued. "We will travel back out into the Galaxy and seek new experiences; new strands to be woven into the greater tapestry of the Gentian collective memory. None of us will leave here the same person he or she was a thousand days ago, and when we return, we will have changed again. That is part of the wonder of what Abigail made of herself. Other Lines favour rigid regimentation: a thousand identical clones, each programmed to respond to the same stimulus in exactly the same way. You might as well send out robots. That wasn't how Abigail wanted to do things. She wanted to gorge on reality. She wanted to feed her face with it, drunk on curiosity. In our bickering diversity, we honour that impulse." I paused and laced my hands, nodding at the nearest faces. "And now the time has come. The system has informed me of the winner… the name I am about to reveal." I pulled a face that suggested amused surprise. "The name is…"

And then I paused again, and frowned. The crowd tensed.

"Wait a moment," I said. "I'm sorry, but…something's wrong. I'm receiving an emergency message from my ship." I raised my voice over the people who had started talking. "This is…unfortunate. My ship has a technical problem with drive containment. There's a small but non-negligible risk of detonation." I tried to sound panicked, but still in some kind of control. "Please, remain calm. I'm ordering my ship to move to a safe distance…" I looked over the heads, beyond the island to the forest of parked ships, and counted to five in my head. "No response…I'm trying again, but…" The heads started moving, their voices threatening to drown me out. "Still no response,"

Easily done, I thought. All I would have needed to do is shove a comet onto the right orbit, shatter it and let its dusty tail intersect the orbit of my planet at the right point in space and time...here, tonight. Now that I thought of that, there was a twinge of familiarity about it...the memory of doing so not completely erased.

By the standards of some, it was very low-key, and for a moment I wondered if I had misjudged the effect...but just as I was beginning to worry about that, people started clapping. It was polite at first, but soon it built in enthusiasm, even as the stars quickened their display, flashing overhead too quickly to count.

They liked it.

"Bravo, Campion!" I heard someone say. "Tasteful restraint...beautifully simple!"

I stepped onto a low plinth, so that I was head and shoulders above the crowd. I forced a smile and waved down the applause. "Thank you everyone," I said. "I'm glad things have gone so well. If this reunion has been a success, it has far more to do with the people than the venue." I looked over my shoulder, at the central spire rising behind me. "Although the venue isn't half bad, is it?" They laughed and applauded, and I smiled again, hoping I looked and sounded genuine. It was hard, but it was vital that no one suspect I had anything else up my sleeve.

"Every strand is to be treasured," I said, injecting a note of solemnity into my voice. "Every experience, every memory, is sacred. On this Thousandth Night, we gather to select one strand in particular that has touched us more than others. That is our custom. But in doing so, we do not denigrate any other strands. In the totality of experience, they are all equally vital, and all equally cherished." I singled out Mullein, and smiled sympathetically. "Even the ones with an unusually high mud content."

been honoured with the design of the next venue. Whoever it was, I wished them well. As I had discovered, the praise burned off very quickly, and what was left was a dark, ominous clinker of responsibility.

I looked down on the assembled gathering from a much higher balcony, watching the masked and costumed figures slow in their orbits. The atmosphere of the revellers became perceptibly tense, as my announcement drew nearer. There was a palpable sadness amongst all the gaiety. Friendships made here must be put on hold until the next reunion, two hundred thousand years in the future. Time and space would change some of us. We would not all be the same people, and not all of those friendships would endure.

It was time.

I stepped from the side of my balcony, into open space. There was a collective gasp from the revellers, even though no one seriously expected me to come to harm. As my left foot pushed down into thin air, a sheet of white marble whisked under it to provide support. As my right foot stepped below my left, another sheet whisked under that one. I took weight from my left foot and stepped down again, and the first sheet curved back under me to meet my falling foot. Stepping between these two sheets, I walked calmly down to the lower balcony. The effect was everything I could have wished for, and I tried to look as quietly pleased with myself as I ought to have been.

But not all the eyes were upon me. Masked and unmasked faces were caught by something above. I followed their gaze to see another slashing shooting star, and then another. In quick succession, six more cut the sky from zenith to horizon. Then more. A dozen in the first minute, and then two dozen in the second. I smiled, realising that this must be the surprise I had arranged for Thousandth Night. A meteor shower!

or otherwise, reflected the content of their dream. We wore carnival masks, the game being to match the dreamer to the dream before the masks were ripped away. I wore a moon mask and a simple outfit patterned in sunset shades, with a repeating motif of half-swallowed suns. Purslane wore a fox mask and a harlequin costume, in which each square detailed one of her legendary adventures. It didn't take very long for people to work out who she was. Once again, she was tormented by questions about the false strand, but she only had to keep up the pretence for a few more hours. Soon our deception would be revealed, and we would beg forgiveness for weaving a lie.

"Look," I heard someone say, pointing to the zenith. "A shooting star!"

I looked up sharply enough to catch the etched trail before it faded from sight. A shooting star, I thought: a good omen, perhaps. Except I didn't believe in omens, especially not when they were signified by pieces of cosmic grit slamming into our planet's atmosphere.

Purslane sidled up to me a few minutes later. "Are you sure you want to go through with this?"

"Yes. In less than a day, every ship you see here will be on its way out of the system. We do it now or we forget about it forever."

"Maybe that would be easier."

"Easier, yes. The right thing—no."

Another shooting star slashed the sky.

"I agree," she said.

Upon midnight, the revellers assembled on a high balcony flung out from the side of the main tower on an arm of curved ivory. They had all cast their votes and my system had tallied the winning strand. Shortly it would push the information into my head, and I would deliver the much-anticipated announcement. One of us would leave the system heady with the knowledge their dream had moved us like no other, and that they had and wonders, and perhaps a little mud along the way. Our knowledge of the galaxy we called home had accreted yet another layer of detail, even as the endless transformations of history rendered much of that knowledge obsolete. For most of us, it was of no concern. The innate fascination of the strands, the spectacle, intrigue, and glamour of this final evening together was all that mattered. Not the Advocates, though. Though they did their best to hide it, they itched with impatience. For two million years, they had accepted the crushing scale of the galaxy and their own fixed relationship to that immensity. When Abigail Gentian shattered herself into nine hundred and ninety-nine gemlike pieces, she had hoped to conquer space and time. Instead, she had only come to a deeper understanding of her own microscopic insignificance. The Advocates could not tolerate that any longer.

I kept a stiff, strained smile on my face as I made my rounds of the Thousandth Night revellers, accepting compliments. Although my strand had not set the world on fire, no one had any serious complaints about the venue. The island was just the right size: small enough to feel intimate, but with enough curious little byways and quirks of design not to become boring. Every now and then I had introduced some minor change—moving a passage here, or a staircase there, and my efforts were generally deemed to have been worthwhile. The white terraces, balconies and bridges of the island had a charm of their own, but they had not detracted from the strands, and the threadings had gone flawlessly. Time and again, people squeezed my sleeve and asked me what I had lined up for the final night, and time and again I confessed that I couldn't even be sure that I *had* lined anything up at all.

Of course, I knew I must have planned something.

Evening turned to night. Floating paper lanterns glowed in the warm air, casting lozenges of pastel color on the revellers. As was Gentian custom, everyone wore a costume that, subtly

I paused and let those numbers crunch against each other. "Better. Now we're down to...what? Seven or eight ships, depending on where you draw the cut-off for the size estimate. Seven or eight names. One of which happens to be Fescue."

"Still not good enough, though."

I thought for a moment. "If we could narrow it down to one ship...then we'd be sure, wouldn't we?"

"That's the problem, Campion. We can't narrow it down. Not unless we saw what those anticollision fields looked like."

"Exactly," I said. "If we could get them to put up their screens...all we'd need to do is find the ship with the closest resonance to the one in Grisha's system."

"Wherever you're taking this line of thought..." Purslane's eyes flashed a warning at me.

"All I need to do is find a way to get them to trigger their shields. Full ship screens, of course."

"It won't work. If they get an inkling of what you're up to, they'll tune to a different resonance."

"Then I'd better not give them much warning," I said. "We'll do it on Thousandth Night, just the way we said we would. They'll be too distracted to plan anything in advance, and they won't be expecting a last minute surprise."

"I like the way you say 'we'."

"We're in this together now," I said. "All the way. Even if we take the line with us."

Purslane sniffed her wineglass. "How are you going to get everyone to turn on their shields?"

I squinted against the sun. "I'm sure I'll think of something."

Because I was dreading its arrival, Thousandth Night was suddenly upon us. Since Purslane's discovery that Burdock had lied, the reunion had passed by in a blur. For nine hundred and ninety-nine nights we had dreamed of suns and worlds, miracles

I closed my eyes and directed a command at my own ship. "Me too. Want to take a bet on who finds something first?"

"No point, Campion. I'd thrash you."

She did, too. Her ship found something almost immediately, now that it had been given the right search criteria. "It's still at the limits of detection," she said. "They must have had their screens tuned right down, for just this reason. But they couldn't run with them turned off."

"Is this enough to narrow it down?"

"Enough to improve matters. The resonant frequency of the graviton pulse is at the low end: that means whoever's doing this was throwing up a big screen."

Like blowing a low note in a big bottle, rather than a high note in a small bottle.

"Meaning big ship," I said.

"I'm guessing fifty or sixty kilometers at the minimum." She looked at the parade of hanging ships. "That already narrows it down to less than a hundred."

My ship pushed a memory into my head: a girl seated in the lotus position, with a golden, glowing cube rotating above her cupped palms. It meant that the ship had a result.

"Mine's in," I said, requesting a full summary. "My ship says seventy kilometers at the low end, with a central estimate around ninety. See: slow, but she gets there in the end."

"My ship's refined its analysis and come to more or less the same conclusion," Purslane said. "That narrows it down even more. We're talking about maybe twenty ships."

"Still not good enough," I said ruefully. "We can't point fingers unless we have a better idea than that."

"Agreed. But we have the drive flame as an additional constraint. Not all of those twenty ships even use visible thrust. And we also know who Burdock spoke to about the Great Work."

he put the moon back together again and (this was a touch of genius, we had to admit) he *wrote his signature* on the back of the tide-locked moon in a chain of craters. It was flashy, completely contrary to any number of Line strictures, but it got people talking about Borage, not Purslane.

I could have kissed the egomaniacal bastard.

"I think we got away with that one," I told Purslane, when she was finally able to move through the island without being pestered by an entourage of hangers-on.

"Good," she said. "But that doesn't mean we're any closer to finding out who killed Grisha's people."

"Actually," I said, "I've been thinking about that. Maybe there's something in that data after all."

"We've been through it with a fine-toothed comb."

"But looking for the obvious signatures," I said.

"There are too many gaps."

"But maybe the gaps are telling us something. What caused the gaps?"

"Burdock being too cautious, throwing up his screens every time a speck of dust came within a light-second of his ship. His screens are sensor-opaque, at least in all the useful bands."

"Correct. But some of those activations were probably necessary: there *was* a lot of rubble, after all."

"Go on," she said.

"Well, if there was a lot of debris that far out, there must have been even more closer to the action. Enough to trigger the screens of the other ship."

"I hadn't thought of that."

"Me neither, until now. And the type of search we've been doing wouldn't have picked up screen signatures. We need to slice the data up into short time windows and filter on narrow-band graviton pulses. *Then* we might find something."

"I'm already on it," Purslane said.

"That's sort of the reaction we were hoping for. The one thing no one will be wondering about is what you were up to last night. And we can be sure no one ducked out of the strand."

"What about Burdock's impostor? We didn't know about him when we hatched this plan."

"He still had to act like Burdock," I said. "That means he'll have needed to dream your strand."

"I hope you're right."

"You only have to get through this one day. It's Squill's strand tonight. He always gives good dream."

Purslane looked at me pityingly. "Keep up, Campion. Squill's been off-form for half a million years."

Unfortunately, she was right about Squill. His strand consisted of endless visits to planets and artefacts left over from the Interstitial Uprising, overlaid with tedious, self-serving monologues of historical analysis. It was not the hit of the reunion, and it did little to take the heat off Purslane. The next night wasn't much better: Mullein's strand was a workmanlike trudge through thirty cultures that had collapsed back to pre-industrial feudalism. "Mud," I heard someone say dispiritedly, the day after. "Lots of...mud."

The third night was a washout as well. That was when Asphodel would have delivered her strand, had she made it back to the reunion. As was our custom, her contribution took the form of a compilation from her previous strands. It was all very worthy, but not enough to stop people talking about Purslane's exploits.

Thankfully, things picked up for her on the fourth night. Borage's strand detailed his heroic exploits in rescuing an entire planet's worth of people following the close approach of a star to their Oort cloud. Borage dropped replicators on their nearest moon and converted part of it into a toroidal defence screen, shielding their planet from the infall of dislodged comets. Then

Purslane shook her head. "Don't think so. The gaps seem to be caused by his anticollision screens going up, blinding his sensors. You saw how old that ship was: it probably has pretty ancient screen generators, or pretty ancient sensors, or both."

"Why the anticollision screens?"

"Debris," Purslane said. "Grisha's system had been turned into a cloud of radioactive rubble. Burdock's approach never took him all that close to the main action, but there must still have been a lot of debris flying around. If he'd thought to turn up his triggering threshold, he might have given us more to work with…"

I tried to sound optimistic. "We'll just to have make the best of what's left."

"My ship's already made the obvious checks. I've seen the flame Burdock mentioned, but it really is too faint for an accurate match. If the murderers were hanging around the system before then, they must have been very well camouflaged."

"We can't just…give up," I said, thinking of the man we had left behind on Burdock's ship. "We owe it to Burdock, and Grisha, and Grisha's people."

"If there's nothing there, there's nothing there," Purslane said.

She was right. But it wasn't what I wanted to hear.

We landed on the island and reset our body clocks so that—to first approximation—we looked and felt as if we had just passed a restful, dream-filled night. That was the idea, at least. But when I conjured a mirror and examined my face in it I saw a quivering, tic-like tightness around the mouth. I tried a kinesic reset but it didn't go away. When Purslane and I met alone on one of the high balconies, after breakfasting with a few other line members, I swear saw the same tightness.

"How did it go?" I asked.

She kept her voice low. "It was as bad as I feared. They thought my strand was *wonderful, darling.* They won't stop asking me about it. They hate me."

racing outward at sixty kilometers a second. Another memorial, no less heartfelt, had taken the form of a single stone kiln on an airless moon. Both had been appropriate.

Burdock would surely receive his due, but his death had to remain a secret until Thousandth Night. Until then Purslane and I would have to walk among our fellow line members with that knowledge in our hearts, and not betray the slightest hint of it.

We owed it to Burdock.

"We're in time," I said, as the box neared the island. "That took longer than I'd hoped, but the threading is still taking place. No one will have missed us yet."

Purslane pressed a hand to her brow. "God, the threading. I'd forgotten all about that. Now I'll have to spend all day telling lies. Please tell me this was a good idea, Campion."

"Wasn't it? We know what happened to Burdock now. We know about Grisha and the Great Work. *Of course* it was worth it."

"Are you so sure? All we know now is that asking questions could get us into serious trouble. We're still none the wiser about who's actually behind this. I'm not sure I wasn't happier in blissful ignorance."

"We have the data from Burdock's ship," I reminded her.

"Have you looked at it yet, Campion?" I could tell from her tone that she wasn't impressed. "My ship's already sent me back a preliminary analysis. Burdock's data is riddled with gaps."

"He warned us there were a few holes."

"What he didn't say was that thirty percent of his records were missing. There may be something useful in the remaining data, but there's still a good chance that the clues fell into the gaps."

"Why the gaps in the first place? Do you think he edited out something he didn't want us to see?"

Grisha stood by the couch, his gun still in his hand. "Did you learn all that you needed to know?" he asked.

"I think so," I started to say.

"Good," he said. "Because Burdock's dead. He gave you the last minute of his life."

PURSLANE AND I returned to the island as the sky lightened in anticipation of dawn. It was still midnight blue overhead, but the horizon was tinged with the softest tangerine orange, cut through by ribbons of cloud. As the box wheeled through the thicket of hanging ships toward the island I began to see the crests of waves, stippled in brightening gold.

I had seen many dawns, but in all my travels I had never tired of them. Even now, with the weight of all that had happened and all that we had learned, some part of me stood aside from the moment to acknowledge the simple beauty of sunrise on another world. I wondered what Burdock would have made of it. Would it have touched him with the same alchemical force, bypassing the rational mind to speak to that animal part from which we were separated by only an evolutionary heartbeat? Perhaps I'd find a clue in all the strands Burdock had submitted during his time among us. Now there would be no more.

A death among the line was a terrible and rare thing. When it happened, one of us would be tasked to create a suitable memorial somewhere out in the stars. Such a memorial could take many forms. Long ago, the death of one of our number had been commemorated by the seeding of ferrite dust into the atmosphere of a dying star, just before the star expelled its outer envelope to create a nebula in the shape of a human head, sketched in lacy curves of blue green oxygen and red hydrogen, catastrophe. Spread out across tens of thousands of light years, we were immune to extinction, at least by our own hands.

Compactified, death could touch us all in less than five thousand years.

"The Advocates knew this, I think," Burdock said. "But they considered it to be a theoretical problem they would deal with when the time came. Surely, they rationalised, we would be wise enough to avoid such foolishness. But then they learned of the discovery made by the Watchers, and rediscovered by Grisha's people. Another spiral culture that had gone down the same path—and ended up extinct; wiped out in a cosmological instant. Perhaps the fate was not so avoidable after all, no matter how wise you became. By rights, they should have viewed this data as an awful warning, and acted accordingly: abandoning the Great Work before a single star had moved an inch."

But it was never going to happen like that. The lines had already invested too much of themselves in the future success of the Work. Alliances had already been forged; hierarchies of influence and responsibility agreed upon. To back down now would involve crushing loss of face to the senior lines. Old wounds would be reopened; old rivalries would simmer to the fore. If the Great Work was the project that would bind the lines, its abandonment could very easily push some of them to war. That was why Grisha's people had to be silenced, even if it meant their genocide. For what was the loss of one culture, against something so huge? If we were still living in the prologue to history, they would be doing well to merit a footnote.

The vision ended then, and I felt my mind being sucked back to the body I had left (and nearly forgotten) aboard Burdock's ship. There was a moment of unpleasant confinement, as if I was a being squeezed into a too-small bottle, and then I was back, still holding hands with Purslane, the two of us reeling as our inner ears adjusted to the return of gravity.

worlds would be forged, vast as stars themselves: the golden palaces and senates of this new galactic empire. With a light-crossing time of only fifty centuries, something like an empire was indeed possible. History would no longer outpace starfarers like Purslane and I. If we learned of something magical on the other side of human space, there would be every hope that it would still be there when we arrived. And most of humanity would be packed into a light-crossing time much less than fifty centuries.

This was the Great Work. It was the culminative project of two million years of human advancement: the enterprise that would the tax the ingenuity and resourcefulness of the most powerful lines. Where the lines squabbled now, they would come together in peaceful cooperation. And at the end of it (if any of us lived that long), we would have something wonderful to show for it. It would be the ultimate human achievement, a spectacle of engineering visible across cosmological distance. A beacon to our bright monkey cleverness.

It could not be allowed to happen.

That was the message Grisha's people had uncovered, in their archaeological enquiries into their planet's Prior culture. It transpired that the Watchers had witnessed something like the Great Work once already, in the distant spiral galaxy that they had been monitoring. Perhaps it was a kind of recurrent pathology, destined to afflict civilisations once they reached a certain evolutionary state. They grew weary of the scale of their galaxy and sought to shrink it.

In doing so they created the preconditions for their own extinction. Where once they had moved too slowly to threaten more than a handful of neighbouring systems, the compactification allowed war and disease to spread like wildfire. The inhuman scale of the colonised Galaxy was its strength as well as its weakness: time and distance were buffers against

Burdock told us that the Advocates had been covertly resurrecting Prior methods of stellar engineering, contesting them against each other to find the most efficient processes. The methods that worked best seemed to be those that employed some of the star's own fusion power as the prime mover. They used mirrors to direct the star's energy output in a single direction, in the manner of a rocket motor. If the star's acceleration were sufficiently gentle, it would carry its entire family of worlds and rubble and dust with it.

Of all the Prior methods tested so far, none were able to accelerate a sunlike star to anything faster that one percent of the speed of light. This was laughably slow compared to our oldest ships, but it didn't matter to the Advocates. Even if it took two or three more million years to move all their target stars, this was still a price worth paying. Everything that had happened to date, they liked to say, was just a *prologue to history*. Real human affairs would not begin in earnest until the last star was dropped into its designed Galactic orbit. Set against the billions of years ahead of us (before the Galaxy itself began to wither, or suffered a damaging encounter with Andromeda) what was a mere handful of millions of years?

It was like delaying a great voyage by a few hours.

When they were done, the Galaxy would look very different. All life-bearing stars (cool and long-lived suns, for the most part) would have been shunted much closer to the core, until they fell within a volume only five thousand light years across. Superhot blue stars—primed to explode as supernovae in mere millions of years—would be prematurely triggered, or shoved out of harm's way. Unstable binaries would be dismantled like delicate time bombs. The unwieldy clockwork of the central black hole would be tamed and harnessed for human consumption. Stars that were already on the point of falling into the central engine would be mined for raw materials. New

Interesting star systems were thousands or tens of thousands of years of flight time apart. Planetary time moved much faster than that. Human events outpaced the voyagers, so that what they experienced was only glimpses of history, infuriatingly incomplete. Brief, bittersweet golden ages flourished for a handful of centuries while the ships were still moving between stars. Glories went unrecorded, unremembered.

Something had to be done.

"The lines have been gnawing at the lightspeed problem for half a million years," Burdock said. "It won't crack. It's just the way the universe is. Faced with that, you have two other possibilities. You can reengineer human nature to slow history to a crawl, so that starfarers can keep pace with planetary time. Or you can consider the alternative. You can reengineer the Galaxy itself, to shrink it to a human scale."

In an eye blink of comprehension we understood the Great Work, and why it had been necessary for Grisha's people to die. The Great Work concerned nothing less than the relocation of entire stars and all the worlds that orbited them.

Moving stars was not actually as difficult as it sounded. The Priors had moved stars around many times, using many different methods. It had even taken place in the human era: demonstration projects designed to boost the prestige of whichever culture or line happened to be sponsoring it. But the Great Work was not about moving one or two stars a few light years, impressive as such a feat undoubtedly was. The Great Work was about the herding of stars in numbers too large to comprehend: the movement of hundreds of millions of stars across distances of tens of thousand of light years. The Advocates dreamed of nothing less than compactifying the Milky Way; taking nature's work and remaking it into something more useful for human occupation. For quick-witted monkeys, it was no different than clearing a forest, or draining a swamp.

fingerprint. The hundreds of billions of stars formed a blizzard of light, but through some trick of perception I felt that I recognized all the systems I had visited during my travels, as well as all those I had come to know through the shared memories of the Gentian Line. I made out the little yellow sun which we now orbited, and felt both inconsequential and godlike as I imagined myself on a watery world circling that star, a thing tiny beyond measure, yet with an entire galaxy wheeling inside my head.

"You know this place, of course," said Burdock's disembodied voice. "As one facet of Abigail, you've crossed it ten or twelve times; tasted the air of a few hundred worlds. Enough for one lifetime, perhaps. But that was never enough for Abigail, for us. As Abigail's shattered self we've crossed it ten thousand times; known a million worlds. We've seen wonder and terror; heaven and hell. We've seen empires and dynasties pass like seasons. And still that isn't enough. We're still monkeys, you know. In terms of the deep structure of our minds, we've barely left the trees. There's always a shinier, juicier piece of fruit just out of reach. We've reached for it across two million years and it's brought to us this place, this moment. And now we reach again. We embark on our grandest scheme to date: the Great Work."

The view of the Milky Way did not change in any perceptible way, but I was suddenly aware of human traffic crossing between the stars. Ships much like those of the Gentian Line fanned out from points of reunion, made vast circuits across enormous swathes of the Galaxy, and converged back again two or three hundred thousand years later, ready to merge experiences. Cocooned in relativistic time, the journeys did not seem horrendously long for the pilots: mere years or decades of flight, with the rest of time (which might equal many centuries) spent soaking up planetary experience, harvesting memory and wisdom. But the true picture was of crushing slowness, even though the ships moved at the keen, sharp edge of lightspeed.

his story was a lie as well? We had no evidence that Grisha was authentic, and not just a figment created by the ship.

"You have to trust me," Burdock pleaded. "There isn't much time left."

"He's right," Purslane said, gripping my hand. "There's a risk, but there's also a risk in doing nothing. We have to do this."

I nodded at Burdock. "Tell us."

"Prepare," he whispered.

An instant later I felt a kind of mental prickle as something touched my brain, groping its way in like an octopus seeking a way into a shell. Purslane tightened her hold, anchoring herself to me. There was a moment of resistance and then the intrusive thing was ensconced.

My sense of being present in the room became attenuated, as if my body was suddenly at the far end of a long thread of nerve fibres, with my brain somewhere else entirely. I didn't know how Burdock was doing it, but I could see at least two possibilities. The air in his ship might have been thick with machines, able to swim into neural spaces and tap into direct mental processes. Or the ship itself might been generating external magnetic fields of great precision, steering the foci into my skull and stimulating microscopic areas of my mind. I was only dimly aware of Grisha and Burdock looking on, half a universe away.

Coldness seized me, electric with the crackle and fizz of subatomic radiation. I was somewhere dark beyond imagination. My point of view shifted and something awesome hoed into view. As my disembodied eyes adjusted to the darkness, the thing brightened and grew layers of dizzying detail.

It was a spiral galaxy.

I recognized it instantly as the Milky Way. I had crossed it enough times to know the kinked architecture of its stellar arms and dust lanes, a whorl as familiar and idiosyncratic as a

"You had no other means of witnessing events?"

"No. Everything I saw came through the ship's eyes and ears in one form or another."

"That should be good enough. Can you pass those records to my ship?"

"Mine as well," Purslane said.

Burdock waited a moment. "It's done. I'm afraid you'll still have some compatibility issues to deal with."

A coded memory flash—a bee landing on a flower—told me that my ship had just received a transmission from another craft, in an unfamiliar file format. I sent another command to my ship to tell it to start working on the format conversion. I had faith that it would get there in the end: I often set it the task of interpreting Prior languages, just to keep its mental muscles in shape.

"Thank you," I said.

"Make what you will of it. I'm afraid there are many gaps in the sensor data. You'll just have to fill in the holes."

"We'll do what we can," Purslane said. "But if we're to bring anyone to justice, we have to know what this is all about. You must tell us what you've learned of the Great Work."

"I only know parts. I've guessed most of it."

"That's still more than Campion and I know."

"All right," he said, with something like relief. "I'll tell you. But there isn't time to do this the civilised way. Will you give me permission to push imagery into your heads?"

Purslane and I looked at each other uneasily. Rationally, we had nothing to fear: if Burdock had the means to tamper with our heads, he could have already forced hallucinations on us by now, or killed us effortlessly. We willingly opened our memories during each threading, but that was within the solemn parameters of age-old ceremony, when we were all equally vulnerable. We already knew Burdock had lied once. What if the rest of

Abigail valued death as much as she valued life. Though we were all technically immortal, that immortality only extended to our cellular processes. If we destroyed our bodies, we died. Gentian protocol forbade backups, or last minute neural scans. She wanted her memories to burn bright with the knowledge that life—even a life spanning hundreds of thousands of years—was only a sliver of light between two immensities of darkness.

Burdock would die. Nothing in the universe could stop that now.

"When you witnessed the crime," I said, "did you see anything that could tell us who was responsible?"

"I've been through my memories of my passage through Grisha's system thousand times," he said. "After I rescued Grisha, I caught a trace of a drive flame exiting the system in the opposite direction. Presumably whoever deployed the machines was still around until then, making sure that the job was done."

"We should be able to match the drive signature to one of the ships parked here," I said.

"I've tried, but the detection was too faint. There's nothing that narrows down my list of suspects."

"Maybe a fresh pair of eyes might help, though," Purslane said. "Or even two pairs."

"Direct exchange of memories is forbidden outside of threading," Burdock said heavily.

"Add it to the list of Gentian rules we've already broken tonight," I said. "Falsification of Purslane's strand, absence from the island during a threading, breaking into someone else's ship…why don't you let *me* worry about the rules, Burdock? My neck's already on the line."

"I suppose one more wrong won't make much difference," he said, resignedly. "The sensor records of my passage through Grisha's system are still in my ship files—will they be enough?"

"I suppose so," Burdock said, with not quite the conviction I might have hoped for. "Does it look like I have a great deal of choice?"

"We're not implicated," Purslane said soothingly. "But we are concerned to expose the truth."

"It's dangerous. Everything I said still holds. They'll take this world apart to safeguard the Great Work. Unless you can organise a significant number of allies and move against them quickly...I fear they'll gain the upper hand."

"Then we'll just have to outplay them, so that they never get a chance." Easier said than done, I thought. We had no more idea who we could trust than Burdock himself.

"Whatever we do," Purslane said, "it'll have to happen before Thousandth Night. If there's any evidence pointing to a crime now, it'll be lost forever by the time we return here."

"She's right," I said. "If Gentian Line is implicated, then whoever's involved is on the island now. That gives us something. We've at least got them in one place."

"Thousandth Night would be a good time to move," Purslane mused. "If we leave it until then—the last possible moment—they'll probably have assumed nothing's going to happen."

"Risky," I said.

"It's all risky. At least that way we stand a chance of catching them off guard. There's only one thing anyone ever thinks about on Thousandth Night."

"Purslane may have a point," Burdock said. "Whoever the perpetrators are, they're still part of the line. They'll be waiting to see who wins best strand, just like the rest of you."

I noticed that he said "you" rather than "us." On his deathbed, Burdock had already begun the process of abdication from Gentian affairs. Knowing he would not see Thousandth Night, let alone another reunion, he was turning away from the line.

"Obviously my idea of subtle wasn't *their* idea of subtle. Well, it proves I was onto something, I suppose. At least one of our line has to be involved."

I tapped a finger against my nose. "Why didn't they just kill you on the island, and be done with it?"

"It was *your* island, Campion. How would they have killed me without you noticing it? Administering a poisonous agent was simpler—at least that way they didn't have a body to dispose of."

"Do you know about the impostor?" I asked.

"My ship kept a watch on the island. More than once I saw myself strolling on the high promenades."

"You could have signalled us," Purslane said. "Made your ship malfunction, or something like that."

"No. I thought of that, of course. But if my enemies had the slightest suspicion I was still alive, they might have attacked the ship. Remember: they poisoned me not because I knew what had happened, but simply because I was asking too many questions. It's entirely possible that they've done this to other line members in the past. There might be other impostors on your island, Campion."

"I'd know," I said automatically.

"Would you? Would you really?"

When he put it like that, I wasn't sure. I wasn't in the habit of looking inside the skulls of other line members, just to make sure they were really who I assumed them to be. Mental architecture was a private thing at the best of times. And a strand was a strand, whether it was delivered by a thinking person or a mindless duplicate.

"You could have sent a message to one of us," Purslane said.

"How would I have known you were to be trusted? From where I was sitting, hardly anyone wasn't a possible suspect."

"Do you trust us now?" I asked.

"Not really. Whoever was behind this had murdered those people because of something big, and the only big thing I could think of was the Work. What else do the Advocates talk about, Campion—other than their own inflated sense of self-worth?"

"You have a point."

"Anyway, the more I dug, the more it looked like I was right about that hunch. It did tie in with the Work. But I still didn't have any names. I thought if I could at least isolate the line members who had the strongest ties to the Work, then I could start looking for flaws in their strands…"

"Flaws?" Purslane asked.

"Yes. At least one of them had to have been near Grisha's system at the same time as me. They won't have used intermediaries for that kind of thing."

But it was only good luck that we had found the flaw in Burdock's strand in the first place, I thought. Even if someone else had fabricated all or part of their strand, there was no reason to assume they had made the same kind of mistake.

"Did you narrow it down to anyone?" Purslane asked.

"A handful of plausible suspects…conspicuous Advocates, for the most part. I'm sure you could draw up the same shortlist with little effort."

I thought of the Advocates I knew, and the one in particular I had never liked. "Was Fescue among them?"

"Yes," Burdock said. "He was one of them. No love lost there, I see."

"Fescue is a senior Advocate," Purslane said. "He's tried to keep Campion and I apart. It could easily be that he knows we're onto something. If anyone has the means…"

"There are others besides Fescue. I needed to know who it was. That was why I started asking questions, nosing around, trying to goad someone into an indiscretion."

"We noticed," I said.

"Gentian, or one of our allies. I had witnessed a terrible crime, a genocide worse than anything recorded in our history."

"Why did you cover it up?" Purslane asked.

"The knowledge frightened me. But that wasn't the reason I altered my strand. I did it because I needed time: time to identify those responsible, and protect Grisha from them until I had enough evidence to bring them to justice. If the perpetrators were among us—and I had reason to think they were—they would have killed Grisha to silence him. And if killing Grisha meant killing the rest of us, I don't think they'd have blinked at that." He managed a despairing laugh. "When you've just wiped out a two-million-year-old civilisation, what do a thousand clones matter?"

I tried not to sound too disbelieving. "The murder of an entire line? You think they'd go that far, just to cover up an earlier crime?"

"And more," Burdock said gravely. "This is about more than our piddling little line, Campion."

"The Great Work," Purslane said, voicing my own thoughts. "A project bigger than any single line. That's what they killed for, isn't it. And that's what they'll kill for again."

"You're good," Burdock said. "I couldn't have asked for a better pair of amateur sleuths."

"We still don't know anything about the Great Work itself," I told him. "Or why Grisha's people had to die."

"I'll tell you about the Work in good time. First we need to talk about the people who want Grisha dead."

Purslane looked at the other man, and then returned her attention to Burdock. "Do you know their names?"

"It was names I was after," he said. "I had a suspicion—little more than a hunch—that the genocide had something to do with the Work."

"Quite a hunch," I commented.

quality of that consciousness degrading as the weapon gorged itself on his mind.

"I was hoping someone would make it this far," Burdock said, opening his eyes. He didn't turn his head to greet us—the consuming plaque would have made that all but impossible even if he had the will—but I assumed that he had some other means of identifying us. His lips barely moved, but something was amplifying his words, or his intention to speak. "I know how you broke into my ship," he said, "and I presume Grisha's told you something of his place in this whole mess."

"A bit," I said.

"That's good—no need to go over that again." The words had their own erratic rhythm, like slowly dripping water. "But what made you come out here in the first place?"

"There was a discrepancy in your strand," Purslane said, approaching uncomfortably close to the bedside screen. "It conflicted with Campion's version of events. One of you had to be lying."

"You said you'd been somewhere you hadn't," I said. "I happened to be there at the same time, or else no one would ever have known."

"Yes," he said. "I lied; submitted a false strand. Most of it was true—you probably guessed that much—but I had to cover up my visit to Grisha's system."

I nodded. "Because you knew who had destroyed Grisha's people?"

"The weapons were old: million year old relics from some ancient war. That should have made them untraceable. But I found one of the weapons, adrift and deactivated. New control systems had been grafted over the old machinery. These control systems used line protocols."

"Gentian?"

Most had died immediately, but there had been enough warning for a handful of people to abandon the ship in smaller vehicles. Most of those had been picked off, as well. But Grisha had made it. He had fallen out of his system, engines dead, systems powered down to a trickle of life-support. And still he hadn't been dark or silent enough to avoid detection.

But this time it wasn't the machines that found him. It was another ship—a Gentian Line vessel that just happened to be passing by.

Burdock had pulled him out of the escape craft; warmed him from the emergency hibernation, and cracked the labyrinth of his ancient language.

Then Burdock taught Grisha how to speak his own tongue.

"He saved my life," Grisha said. "We fled the system at maximum thrust, outracing the machines. They tried to chase us, and for a little while it seemed that they had the edge. But eventually we made it."

Even as I framed the question, I think I already had an inkling of the answer. "These machines...the ones that murdered your people?"

"Yes," Grisha said.

"Who sent them?"

He looked at both of us and said, very quietly, "You did."

O←

WE WOKE BURDOCK.

The assassination toxin was eating him at a measurable rate; cubic centimeters per hour at normal body temperatures. With Burdock cooled below consciousness, the consumption was retarded to a glacially slow attack. But he would have to be warmed to talk to us, and so his remaining allowance of conscious life could be defined in a window of minutes, with the

"And then?" I asked.

"Then...they did something about it." Grisha opened his mouth as if to speak more on the matter, then seemed to think better of it. "The Watchers continued to study the spiral culture. They gathered data, and when the Watchers passed away, that same data was entombed on the first world that my people settled. In the course of our study, we found this data and eventually we learned how to understand it. And for hundreds of thousands of years we thought no more of it: just one observational curiosity among the many gathered by our Priors."

"What did the spiral culture do?" I asked.

"Burdock can tell you that. It'll be better coming from him."

"You were going to tell us how you ended up on his ship," Purslane prompted.

Grisha looked at the recumbent figure, trapped within those trembling fields. "I'm here because Burdock saved me," he said. "Our culture was murdered. Genocide machines took apart our solar system world by world. We made evacuation plans, of course; built ships so that some of us might cross space to another system. We still knew nothing of relativistic starflight, so those ships were necessarily slow and vulnerable. That was our one error. If there was one piece of knowledge we should have allowed ourselves, it was how to build faster ships. Then perhaps, I wouldn't be speaking to you now. Too many of us would have reached other systems for there to be any need for this subterfuge. But as it is, I'm the only survivor."

His ship had crawled away from the butchered system with tens of thousands of refugees aboard. They had stealthed the ship to the best of their ability, and for a little while it looked as if they might make it into interstellar space unmolested. Then an instability in their narrow, shielded fusion flame had sent a clarion across tens of light hours.

The machines were soon on them.

One day it found what it was looking for.

At a surprisingly high redshift, the Eye detected a single spiral galaxy that was alive with intelligence. Judging by the signals emerging from the galaxy—accidental or otherwise—the ancient spiral was home to a single starfaring culture two or three million years into its dominion. The culture might have begun life as several distinct emergent intelligences that had amalgamated into one, or it might have arisen on a single world. At this distance in time and space, it hardly mattered.

What was clear was that the culture had reached a plateau of social and technological development. They had colonised every useful rock in their galaxy, to the point where their collective biomass exceeded that of a large gas giant. They became expert in the art of stellar husbandry: tampering in the nuclear burning processes of stars to prolong their lifetime, or to fan them to hotter temperatures. They shattered worlds and remade them into artful, energy-trapping forms. They played with matter and elemental force the way a child might play with sand and water. There was nothing they couldn't conquer, except time and distance and the iron barrier of the speed of light.

At this point in Grisha's story, Purslane and I looked at each other in a moment of dawning recognition.

"Like us," we both said.

Grisha favoured this assessment with a nod. "They were like you in so very many ways. They desired absolute omniscience. But the sheer scale of the galaxy always crushed them. They could never know everything: only out of date snapshots. Entire histories slipped through their fingers, unwitnessed, unmourned. Like you, they evolved something like the great lines: flocks of cloned individuals to serve as independent observers, gathering information and experience that would later be merged into the collective whole. And like you they discovered that it was only half a victory."

eleven billion years by the time the Watchers learned its age. And yet the study of the stellar populations in spiral galaxies at different redshifts established that the preconditions for the emergence of intelligent life had been in place for several billion years before the Watchers had evolved, even in the most conservative of scenarios.

Were they therefore the first intelligent culture in the universe, or had sentience already arisen in one of those distant spirals?

To answer this question, the Watchers had taken one of their worlds and shattered it to molecular rubble. With the materials thus liberated, they had constructed a swarm of miraculous eyes: a fleet of telescopes that outnumbered the stars in the sky. They had wrapped this fleet around their system and quickened it to a kind of slow, single-minded intelligence. The telescopes peered through the hail of local stars out into intergalactic space. They shared data across a baseline of tens of light hours, sharpening their acuity to the point where they approximated a single all-seeing eye as wide as a solar system.

It took time for light to reach the Eye from distant galaxies. The further out the Eye looked, the further it looked back into the history of the universe. Galaxies ten million light years away were glimpsed as they were ten million years earlier; those a billion light years away offered a window into the universe when it was a billion years younger than the present epoch.

The Eye looked at a huge sample of spiral galaxies, scrutinising them for signs of intelligent activity. It looked for signals across the entire electromagnetic spectrum; it sifted the parallel data streams of neutrino and gravity waves. It hunted for evidence of stellar engineering, of the kind that other Priors had already indulged in: planets remade to increase their surface area, stars sheathed in energy-trapping shells, entire star systems relocated from one galactic region to another.

"This is about more than just Gentian Line," Grisha said. "The loss of a single line would be a setback, but not a crippling one. The other lines would take up the slack. It wouldn't stop the Great Work."

I looked at him. "What do you know about the Great Work?"

"Everything," he said.

"Are you going to tell us?" Purslane asked.

"No," he said. "I'll leave that to Burdock. He still has several minutes of effective consciousness left, and I think he'd rather tell you in person. Before I wake him, though, it might not hurt if I told you a thing or two about myself, and how I came to be here."

"We've got all evening," I said.

GRISHA'S PEOPLE WERE archaeologists. They had been living in the same system for two million years, ever since settling it by generation ark. They had no interest in wider galactic affairs, and seemed perfectly content with a mortal lifespan of a mere two hundred years. They occupied their days in the diligent, monkish study of the Prior culture that had inhabited their system before their own arrival, in the time when humanity was still a gleam in evolution's eye.

The Priors had no name for themselves except the Watchers. They had been hard-shelled, multi-limbed creatures that spent half their lives beneath water. Their biology and culture was alien enough for a lifetime of study: even a modern one. But although they differed from Grisha's people in every superficial respect, there were points of similarity between the two cultures. They too were archaeologists, of a kind.

The Watchers had chosen to focus on a single, simple question. The universe had already been in existence for more than

"He had no choice," Grisha answered. "When he arrived here, the ship detected the contagion and refused to let him leave."

"Noble of it," I said.

"He'd programmed it that way. I think he had a suspicion his enemies might try something like this. If he was infected, he didn't want to be allowed to return and spread it around. He was thinking of the rest of you."

Purslane and I were quiet for a few moments. I think we were both thinking the same rueful thoughts. We had never considered the possibility that Burdock might be acting honourably, even heroically. No matter what else I learned that evening, I knew that I had already misjudged someone who deserved better.

"All the same," I said, "that still doesn't explain why he didn't alert the rest of us. If he knew he'd been poisoned, and if he had half an idea as to who might have been behind it, there'd have been hell to pay."

"Doubtless there would have been," Grisha said. "But Burdock knew the risk was too great."

"Risk of what?" asked Purslane.

"My existence coming to light. If his enemies learned of my existence, learned of what I know, they'd do all in their power to silence me."

"You mean they'd kill you as well?" I asked.

Grisha gave off a quick, henlike cluck of amusement. "Yes, they'd certainly kill me. But not *just* me. That wouldn't be thorough enough. They wouldn't stop at this ship, either. They'd destroy every ship parked around the island, and then the island, and then perhaps the world."

I absorbed what he had said with quiet horror. Again, there was no doubt as to the truth of his words.

"You mean they'd murder all of us?"

"He's been poisoned. It's some kind of assassination weapon: very subtle, very slow, very deadly." Grisha leaned over and stroked the containment bubble, his fingertips pushing flickering pink dimples into the field. "This is more for your benefit than mine. If his contagion touched me, all I'd have to show for it is a nasty rash. It would kill you the same way it's killing him."

"No," I said. "He's Gentian. We can't be killed by an infection."

"It's a line weapon. It's made to kill the likes of you."

"Who did this to him?" Purslane asked. "You, Grisha?"

The question seemed not to offend him. "No, I didn't do this. It was one of *you*—an Advocate, he thought."

I frowned at the silver-ridden corpse. "Burdock told you who did it?"

"Burdock had his suspicions. He couldn't be sure who exactly had poisoned him."

"I don't understand. What exactly happened? How can Burdock be sick here, if we've seen him running around on the island only a couple of hours ago?"

Grisha smiled narrowly: the first hint of emotion to have troubled his face since our introduction. "That wasn't Burdock that you saw. It was a construct, a mimic, created by his enemies. It replaced the real Burdock nearly three weeks ago. They poisoned him before he returned to his ship."

I looked at Purslane and nodded. "If Grisha's telling the truth, that at least explains the change in Burdock's behaviour. We thought he'd been scared off asking any more questions about the Great Work. Instead he'd been supplanted."

"So he did ask too many questions," Purslane said. She creased her forehead prettily. "Wait, though. If he knew he'd been poisoned, why didn't he tell the rest of us? And why did he stay aboard the ship, out of sight, when his impostor was running around on the island?"

A WINDOWLESS ROOM lay near the core of the ship. It was, I realised, the sleeping chamber: the place where the ship's occupants (even if they only amounted to a single person) would have entered metabolic stasis for the long hops between stars. Some craft had engines powerful enough to push them so close to the speed of light that time dilation squeezed all journeys into arbitrarily short intervals of subjective time, but this was not one of those. At the very least Burdock would have had to spend years between stars. For that reason the room was equipped with the medical systems needed to maintain, modify and rejuvenate a body many times over.

And there *was* a body. A pale form, half eaten by some form of brittle, silvery calcification—a plaque that consumed his lower body to the waist, and which had begun to envelope the side of his chest, right shoulder and the right side of his face. A bustle of ivory machines attended the body, which trembled behind the distorting effect of a containment bubble.

"You can look," Grisha said.

We looked. Purslane and I let out a joint gasp of disbelief. The body on the couch belonged to Burdock.

"It doesn't make any sense," I said, studying the recumbent, damaged form. "The body he has on the island is intact. Why keep this failing one alive?"

"That isn't a duplicate body," Grisha said, nodding at the half-consumed form. "That's his only one. That *is* Burdock."

"No," I said. "Burdock was still on the island when we left."

"That wasn't Burdock," Grisha said, with a weary sigh. He pointed the gun at a pair of seats next to the bed. "Sit down, and I'll try and explain."

"What's wrong with him?" Purslane asked, as we followed Grisha's instruction.

"That's nothing to be proud of," the man said. "Not where I come from. If Abigail Gentian was here now, I'd put a hole in her you could piss through."

The dead calm with which he made this statement erased any doubt that he meant exactly what he said. I felt an existential chill. The man would have gladly erased not just Abigail but her entire line.

It was a strange thing to feel despised.

"Who are you?" Purslane asked. "And how do you know Burdock?"

"I'm Grisha," the man said. "I'm a survivor."

"A survivor of what?" I asked. "And how did you come to be aboard Burdock's ship?"

The man looked at me, little in the way of expression troubling his rounded face. Then by some hidden process he seemed to arrive at a decision.

"Wait here," he said. "I'll be back in a moment."

He let go of the particle gun. Instead of dropping to the floor the weapon simply hung exactly where he had left it, with its barrel still aimed in our general direction. Grisha stepped through the door and left the command deck.

"I knew this was a mistake," Purslane whispered. "Do you think that thing is really…"

I moved a tiny distance away from Purslane and the gun flicked its attention onto me. I drew breath and returned to my former spot, the gun following my motion.

"Yes," I said.

"I thought so."

Grisha returned soon enough. He closed his hand around the gun and lowered it a little. It was no longer trained on us, but we were still in Grisha's power.

"Come with me," he said. "There's someone you need to meet."

"I will use this," the man said, "so please do as I say. Move to the middle of the room, away from any instruments."

Purslane and I did as he said, joining each other side by side. I looked at the man, trying to fit him into the Burdock puzzle. By baseline standards his physiological age was mature. His face was lined, especially around the eyes, with flecks of grey in his hair and beard. Something about the way he deported himself led me to believe that he was just as old as he looked. He wore a costume of stiff, skin-tight fabric in a shade of fawn, interrupted here and there by metal plugs and sockets. A curious metal ring encircled his neck.

"We don't know who you are," I said. "But we haven't come to do you any harm."

"Interfering with this ship doesn't count as doing harm?" He spoke the Gentian tongue with scholarly precision, as if he had learned it for this occasion.

"We were just after information," Purslane said.

"Were you now? What kind?"

Purslane flashed me a sidelong glance. "We may as well tell the truth, Campion," she said quietly. "We won't have very much to lose."

"We wanted to know where this ship had been," I said, knowing she was right but not liking it either.

The man jabbed the barrel of the particle gun in my direction. "Why? Why would you care?"

"We care very much. Burdock—the rightful owner of this ship—seems not to have told the truth about what he was up to since the last reunion."

"That's Burdock's business, not yours."

"Do you know Burdock?" I asked, pushing my luck.

"I know him very well," the man told me. "Better than you, I reckon."

"I doubt it. He's one of us. He's Gentian flesh."

of primary colors. "No time to go through it all now," she said. "I'll just commit it to eidetic memory and review it later." She increased the flow of data, until it blurred into whiteness.

I paced nervously up and down the crescent window. "Fine by me. Just out of interest, what are the chances we'll find anything incriminating anyway?"

Purslane's attention snapped onto me for a second. "Why not? We know for a fact that he lied."

"But couldn't he have doctored those logs as well? If he had something to hide...why leave the evidence aboard his ship?"

But Purslane did not answer me. She was looking beyond me, to the door where we had entered. Her mouth formed a silent exclamation of horror and surprise.

"Stop, please," said a voice.

I looked around, all my fears confirmed. But I recognized neither the voice nor the person who had spoken.

It was a man, baseline human in morphology. Nothing about his face marked him as Gentian Line. His rounded skull lacked Abigail's prominent cheekbones, and his eyes were pure matched blue of a deep shade, piercing even in the subdued light of the command deck.

"Who are you?" I asked. "You're not one of us, and you don't look like one of the guests."

"He isn't," Purslane said.

"Step away from the console, please," the man said. His voice was soft, unhurried. The device he held in his fist was all the encouragement we needed. It was a weapon: something unspeakably ancient and nasty. Its barrel glittered with inlaid treasure. His gloved finger caressed the delicate little trigger. Above the grip, defined by swirls of ruby, was the ammonite spiral of a miniature cyclotron. The weapon was a particle gun.

Its beam would slice through us as cleanly as it sliced through the hull of Burdock's ship.

"This is too easy," Purslane said.

"I thought it was meant to be easy. I thought that was the point of going to all that trouble with the access protocol."

"I know," she said. "But it just seems…I was expecting something to slow us down. Now I'm worried that we're walking into a trap."

"Burdock has no reason to set a trap," I said. But I could not deny that I felt the same unease. "Burdock isn't expecting us to visit. He isn't aware that we're onto him."

"Let's check out the command deck," she said. "But let's be quick about it, all right? The sooner we're back on the island, the happier I'll be."

We took the corridor, following its rising, curving ramp through several rotations, obeying signs for the deck all the while. Around us the ship breathed and gurgled like a sleeping monster, digesting its last big meal. Biomechanical constructs were typical products of the Third Intercessionary period, but I had never taken to them myself. I preferred my machines hard-edged, the way nature intended.

But nothing impeded our progress to the command deck. The deck was spaciously laid-out, with a crescent window set into one curve of wall. It looked back across the sea, to the island. A spray of golden lights betrayed the darkening sliver of the main spire. I thought of the dreamers ranged throughout that tower, and of the lies we were peddling them.

Mushroom-shaped consoles studded the floor, rising to waist height. Purslane moved from one to the next, conjuring a status readout with a pass of her hand.

"This is all looks good so far," she said. "Control architecture is much as I remember it from my ship. The navigations logs should be about…here." She halted at one of the mushrooms and flexed her hands in the stiffly formal manner of a dancer. Text and graphics cascaded through the air in a flicker

"We're committed now, Campion. Back on the island they're dreaming my strand and wondering what the hell turned me into such an adventuress. I didn't go to all that trouble to have you back out now."

"All right," I said. "Consider me suitably emboldened."

But though I strove for a note of easy-going jocularity, I could not shake the sense that our adventure had taken a turn into something far more serious. Until this evening all we had done was indulge in harmless surveillance: an indulgence that had added spice to our days. Now we had falsified a strand and were trespassing on someone else's ship. Both deeds were as close to crimes as anything perpetrated within the history of the Gentian Line. Discovery could easily mean expulsion from the line, or something worse.

This was not a game any more.

As we approached the end of the chamber, the constriction at the end eased open with an obscene sucking sound. It admitted warm, wet, pungent air.

We stooped through the low overhang into a much larger room. Like the airlock chamber, it was lit by randomly spaced light nodes, embedded in the fleshy walls like nuts wedged into the bark of a tree. Half a dozen corridors fed off in different directions, labelled with symbols in an obsolete language. I paused a moment while my brain retrieved the necessary reading skills from deep recall.

"This one is supposed to lead to the command deck," I said, as the symbols became suddenly meaningful. "Do you agree?"

"Yes," Purslane said, but with the tiniest note of hesitation in her voice.

"Something wrong?"

"Maybe you're right. Maybe this isn't such a good idea after all."

"What's got you afraid all of a sudden?"

Purslane and I made our move. Two travel boxes folded around us and pulled us away from the island, through the thicket of hanging vessels, out to the ship belonging to Burdock. A kilometer long, it was a modest craft by Gentian standards: neither modern nor fast, but rugged and dependable for all that. Its armored green hull had something of the same semi-translucence as polished turtleshell. Its drive was a veined green bulb, flung out from the stern on a barbed stalk: it hung nose-down from the bulb, swaying gently in the late evening breeze.

Purslane's box led the way. She curved under the frog-like bow of the ship, then rose up on the other side. Halfway up the hull, between a pair of bottle-green hull plates, lay a wrinkled airlock. Her box transmitted recognition protocols and the airlock opened like a gummed eye. There was room inside for both boxes. They opened and allowed us to disembark.

Nothing about Burdock's outward appearance had suggested that the air aboard his ship would be anything but a standard oxygen-nitrogen mix. It was still a relief when I gulped down a lungful and found it palatable. It would have been a chore to have to return to the island and remake my lungs to cope with something poisonous.

"I recognise this design of ship," Purslane said, whispering. We were inside a red-lined antechamber, like a blocked throat. "It's Third Intercessionary. I owned one like it once. I should be able to find my way around it quite easily, provided he hasn't altered too many of the fittings."

"Does the ship know we're here?"

"Oh, yes. But it should regard us as friendly, once we're inside."

"Suddenly this doesn't seem like quite the excellent idea it did ten days ago."

we were doing would have had time to gnaw away at my better judgement. It was a false strand that had set this entire enterprise in motion, I had to remind myself. Burdock had perpetrated a lie, and now we were perpetrating another because of it. Unfortunately, I saw no practical alternative.

Purslane's original strand wasn't as bad as I had feared: there was actually some promising material in it, if only it could be brought out more effectively. It was certainly a lot more dramatic and exciting than my essay on sunsets. Nonetheless, there was plenty of scope for some judicious fiddling with the facts: nothing outrageous, nothing that would have people looking for flaws in Purslane's strand, but enough to justify the anticipation she had begun to stoke. And in that respect she excelled herself: without actually saying anything, she managed to whip everyone into a state of heady expectation. It was all in the haughtiness of her walk, the guarded confidence of her looks, the sympathetic, slightly pitying smile with which she greeted everyone else's efforts. I know she hated every minute of that performance, but to her credit she threw herself into it with giddy abandon. By the time the evening of her threading came around, the atmosphere tingled with excitement. Her strand would be the subject of so much discussion tomorrow that no one could possibly take the risk of not dreaming it tonight, even if my apparatus had permitted such evasion. It would be the most exquisite of embarrassments not to be able to hold a view on Purslane's strand.

At midnight, the line members and their guests dispersed to sleep and dream. Surveillance confirmed that they were all safely under: including, Burdock. The strand was threading into their collective memories. There had been no traffic to and from the island and the ships for an hour. A warm breeze rolled in from the west, but the sea was tranquil, save for the occasional breaching aquatic.

have to talk them up before the thread, so that everyone is in a state of appropriate expectation. Obviously, there's only one person who can do that beforehand. You'll have to drop hints. You'll have to look smug and self-satisfied. You'll have to pour lukewarm praise on someone else's strand."

"Oh, God preserve us from lukewarm praise."

"Trust me," I said. "I know all about that."

She shook her head. "I can't do this, Campion. It isn't me. I don't boast."

"Breaking into ships isn't you either. The rules have changed. We have to be flexible."

"It's all very well you saying that. It's me who's being asked to lie here...and anyway, why do I have to lie in the first place? Are you actually saying you don't think my real strand would be interesting enough?"

"Tell you what," I said, as if the idea had just occurred to me. "Why don't you let me have a look at your strand tonight?. I'll speed-dream the scheduled strand to make room for yours."

"And then what?"

"Then we meet and discuss the material we have to work with. We'll make a few tweaks here and there—heighten this memory, downplay that one. Perhaps exercise a smidgeon of economy with regard to the strict veracity of the events portrayed..."

"Make things up, you mean."

"We need a distraction," I said. "This is the only way, Purslane. If it helps...don't think of it as lying. Think of it as creating a small untruth in order to set free a larger truth. How does that sound?"

"It sounds very dangerous, Campion."

We did it anyway.

Ten days was nowhere as much time as I would have liked, but if we had been given any longer the utter incaution of what the sense in my proposal. "This is our only chance. By Gentian rules, every person on this island is required to receive your strand. With, of course, one exception."

"Me," she said, with a slow, dawning nod. "I don't have to be physically present, since I already know my own memories. But what about…"

"Me? Well, that isn't a problem either. Since I control the apparatus anyway, no one else need know that I wasn't on the island when your strand was threaded."

I watched Purslane's expression as she considered my idea. It was workable: I was convinced of that. I had examined the problem from every conceivable angle, looking for a hairline flaw—and I had found nothing. Well, nothing I could do anything about, anyway.

"But you won't know my strand," Purslane said. "What if someone asks…"

"That isn't a problem, either. Once we've agreed on the strand, I can receive it immediately. I just won't tell anyone until the day after your threading. It'll be just as if I received it the same way as everyone else."

"Wait," Purslane said, raising a hand. "What you just said… about us 'agreeing' on the strand."

"Um, yes?"

"Am I missing something? There isn't anything *to* agree on. I've already prepared and edited my strand to my complete satisfaction. There isn't a single memory I haven't already agonised over a thousand times: putting it in, taking it out again."

"I'm sure you're right," I said, knowing how much of a perfectionist Purslane was. "But unfortunately, we need to make this a tiny bit more of an event."

"I'm not following you, Campion."

"It has to be an effective distraction. Your memories have to be electrifying—the talk of the island for days afterwards. We

"I hope you've given some thought to this," Purslane said.

Well, I had: but I didn't think she was going to like my suggestion overmuch.

"Here's one idea," I said. "I have the entire island under surveillance, so I always know where Burdock is at a given moment, and what he's doing."

"Go on."

"We wait until my systems pick an interval when Burdock's otherwise engaged. An orgy, a game, or a long, distracting conversation..."

Purslane nodded provisionally. "And if he bores of this orgy, or game, or conversation, and extricates himself prematurely?"

"That'll be trickier to handle," I admitted. "But the island is still mine. With some deft intervention I might be able to hold him on the ground for an hour or two before he gets too suspicious."

"That might not be long enough. You can't very well make him a prisoner."

"No, I can't."

"And even if you did manage to keep Burdock occupied for as long as we need, there's the small problem of everyone else. What if someone sees us entering or leaving his ship?"

"That's also a problem," I said. "Which is why that was only suggestion number one. I didn't really think you'd go for it. Are you ready for number two?"

"Yes," she said, with the tone of someone half aware that they were walking into a trap.

"We need a better distraction: one Burdock can't walk away from after an hour or two. We also need one that will keep everyone else tied up—and where *our* absences won't be noticed."

"You've thought of something, haven't you."

"In ten days you deliver your strand, Purslane." I saw a flicker of concern in her face, but I continued, knowing she would see

"Then it isn't just me," I said, relieved that she had shared my observation.

"I wasn't sure whether to say anything. It's not that there's been any dramatic change in his behaviour, just that…"

I completed her sentence for her: an annoying habit I'd spent the last million years trying to break. "…he isn't poking around the Great Work any more."

Purslane's eyes gleamed confirmation. "Exactly."

"Unless I've missed something, he's given up trying to find what it's all about."

"Which tells us one of two possibilities," Purslane said. "Either he thinks he knows enough by now…"

"Or someone has scared him off."

"We really need to take a look at that ship of his," she said. "Now more than ever."

○←

PURSLANE HAD DONE her homework. During one of Burdock's visits to his ship, she had shadowed him with a drone, a glassy dragonfly small and transparent enough to slip undetected into his travel box. The drone had eavesdropped on the exchange of recognition protocols between the box and the hovering ship. A second visit confirmed that the protocol had not changed since the last time: Burdock wasn't using some randomly varying key. There was nothing too surprising about that: we were all meant to be family, after all, and many of the parked ships probably had no security measures at all. It was simply not the done thing to go snooping around without permission.

That was one half of the problem cracked, at least. We could get aboard Burdock's ship, but we would still need to camouflage our departure and absence from the island.

"I suppose you're right," I said, not quite able to suppress my disappointment. The idea of seeing Fescue publicly humiliated—revealed as fabricating chunks of his strand—tasted shamefully delicious.

"Don't let him get to you too much," Samphire said. "He's just a sad old man with too much time on his hands."

"The funny thing," I said, "is that he's no older than the rest of us."

"He *acts* old. That's all that matters."

Samphire's revelation improved my mood, and I took great delight in telling Purslane what I had learned. Robbed of their sting, Fescue's warnings only emboldened the two of us. Time and again, as covertly as we dared, we met aboard her ship and discussed what we had learned.

It was there that I mentioned Burdock's swift passage through the maze.

"He could have been cheating," I said. "His emotional registers were all very flat, according to the maze."

"I don't see why he'd cheat," Purslane answered. "Admittedly, he doesn't have much prestige in the line—but there are other ways he could have won it by now, if it mattered to him that much. It's almost as if he did the maze because he felt obliged to do so…but that it just wasn't difficult for him."

"There's something else, too," I said. "I'm not sure if I'd have noticed it were it not for the whole business with the maze… but ever since then, I've been watching for anything even more out of the ordinary than normal."

"You've seen something?"

"More a case of what he hasn't been doing, rather than what he has been doing, if that makes any sense."

Purslane nodded sagely. "I noticed too—if we're talking about the same thing. It's been going on for at least a week now."

"I doubt it," I said. "But whatever it is, Fescue think it's a lot more important than the kind of lazy, self-indulgent things Purslane and I tend to get up to."

"Has he tried to rope you in?"

"Not sure. I can't work out whether he totally disapproves of me on every level, or whether he's just bitterly disappointed that I waste so much potential talent."

"Well, I wouldn't lose any sleep over it. Fescue's just a wasted old bore. His strand didn't exactly set the island ringing, did it?"

"Nor did mine."

"Difference is Fescue obviously expected more. Between you and me..." Samphire hesitated and looked around. "I think he was just a tiny bit economical with the facts."

I frowned. "You're saying he fiddled his strand?"

"A few details here and there. We came close to meeting around the Hesperus Veil: near enough to exchange recognition protocols."

I nodded. There'd been a supernova near the Hesperus Veil, and a number of us had planned close approaches to it. "That's not enough to prove that he lied, though."

"No," Samphire said. "But according to his strand he skipped the Veil altogether. Why lie about that? Because either before or after that he was somewhere else he didn't want us to know about. Probably somewhere a lot less exciting than the places that showed up in his strand."

I felt a tingling sensation, wondering if Fescue might also be implicated in the Burdock business. Could the two of them be accomplices?

"That's a pretty heavy accusation," I said, my mind reeling.

"Oh, I'm not going to make anything of it. I've already edited down my own strand so as not to embarrass him. Let him trip himself up. He's bound to do it one of these days."

to the exclusion of others. Your sexual relations verge on the monogamous. You spit on the traditions of the line."

I kept my voice level, refusing to rise to his bait. "All this because of a maze, Fescue? I never had you down as quite that bad a loser."

"You have no idea what is at stake," he repeated. "Change is coming, Campion—violent, sudden change. The only thing that will hold the line together is self-sacrifice."

"Is this about the Great Work?" I asked.

"It's about duty," he said. "Something you seem incapable of grasping." He looked back at my maze, as if willing it to crumble to dust. "Keep playing with your toys, Campion. Fritter away your days in idleness and dissipation. Leave the important things to the rest of us."

Fescue stalked off. I stood blinking, regretting the fact that I had mentioned the Great Work. Now my interest in it was known to at least one Advocate.

A hand touched my shoulder. "I see the old fart's giving you a hard time again."

It was Samphire, pushing into my personal space. Normally I would have edged away, but for once I relaxed in his presence, glad to unburden myself.

"I don't think he was thrilled about the Mood Maze," I said.

"Don't take it personally. He's been acting odd for weeks, giving everyone hard stares. What's his problem?"

"Fescue doesn't like me spending time with Purslane."

"Only because the craggy bastard couldn't get a shag out of her."

"I think there's a bit more to it than that. Fescue's mixed up in something. You know what I mean, don't you."

Samphire kept his voice low. "No idea at all. Other than that it's a *work* and it's *great*. Are you any more clued up about it than me?"

maze would tell me something about Burdock's state of mind, if only he would participate. Since it was voluntary, I couldn't be accused of violating his mental privacy.

But when I ran the maze, Burdock sailed through it, with the walls registering hardly any change to his emotional state. Cheating could not be ruled out, though it was unlikely: a Mood Maze was designed to detect most forms of subterfuge and punish them accordingly. And if he had that much to hide, it would not have been hard to avoid the maze entirely.

What surprised me was the degree of frustration I saw in some of the other participants. When a group of Advocates wagered among themselves as to who would beat the maze the quickest, it was Fescue who ended up with the humiliation of being trapped in a closed-loop. His rage built to a crescendo until I tactfully intervened and allowed him an exit.

I greeted him as he left the maze. "Challenging little devil," I said lightly, trying to calm things down.

"A childish little prank," he said, spitting fury. "But then I shouldn't have expected any better from you."

"It's just a game. You didn't have to take part."

"That's all anything is to you, isn't it? Just a game with no consequences." He glanced at the other Advocates, who were looking on with amused expressions. "You have no idea what's at stake here. Even if you did, you'd shrivel from any hint of responsibility."

"All right," I said, holding up my hands in defeat. "I'll forbid you from taking part in any of my games. Will that make you happy?"

"What would make me happy..." Fescue began, before scowling and making to turn away.

"It's Purslane, isn't it," I said.

He lowered his voice to a hiss. "I've given you fair warning. But to what purpose? You continue to associate with her

"I'm afraid so. But don't look so disappointed, Campion. It really doesn't become you."

○←

THEN SOMETHING ODD happened to Burdock. The first hint of it was his flawless navigation of the Mood Maze.

It was customary to sprinkle harmless entertainments and diversions through the nights of the Reunion. On the afternoon of the eight hundred and seventieth night, I opened the maze on one of the high balconies, with a modest prize for the line member who found their way through it the fastest. The maze would remain in existence until the nine hundredth night; time enough for everyone to have a try at it.

But the Mood Maze was no ordinary labyrinth. Based on a game I had discovered during my travels, a Mood Maze was sensitive to emotional states, which the maze detected using a variety of subtle cues and mildly invasive sensors. As long as one remained perfectly calm, a Mood Maze held a fixed geometry. But as soon as the walls detected the slightest suggestion of frustration, the geometry of the maze underwent a sly modification: walls and gaps moving to block one route and open up another. The more frustrated one became, the more tortuous the labyrinth made itself. Extremes of anger could even cause the maze to form a closed-loop around the hapless player, so that they had no choice but to wander in circles until they calmed down. Needless to say, it was considered very bad form to enter a Mood Maze with anything other than baseline human intelligence. Extreme faculties of memory or spatial positioning had to be turned off before participation.

The Mood Maze was a pleasant enough diversion, and popular with most of those who took a chance on it. But I'd had more than that in mind when I set it up. I'd hoped that the

"It must be related to the slowness of interstellar communication," I mused. "That's the fundamental objection, no matter which way you look at it. No signals or ships can cross the Galaxy quickly enough to make any kind of orthodox political system possible. And the lines are too independent to tolerate the kind of social engineering we talked about before. They won't accept any kind of system that imposes limits on human creativity."

"No one takes faster than light travel seriously, Campion."

"It doesn't have to involve travel. A signalling mechanism would be just as useful. We could all stay at home, and communicate via clones or robots. Instead of sending my body to another planet, I'd piggyback a host body that was already there." I shrugged. "Or use sensory stimulation to create a perfect simulation of the other planet and all its inhabitants. Either way, I wouldn't be able to tell the difference. Why would I care?"

"But in two million years," Purslane said, "no culture in the Galaxy has come close to developing faster-than-light communication or travel."

"Lots of people have tried, though. What if some of them succeeded, but kept their breakthrough secret?"

"Or were wiped out to protect the status quo? We can play this game forever. The fact is, faster than light travel—or signalling, for that matter, looks even less likely now than it did a million years ago. The universe simply isn't wired to permit it. It's like trying to play chequers on a chess board."

"You're right of course," I said, sighing. "I studied the mathematics once, for a century. It looks pretty watertight, once you get your head around it. But if that's not the answer..."

"I don't think it is. We should keep open minds, of course... but I think the Great Work has to be something else. What, though, I can't imagine."

"That's as far as you've got?"

"I'm not saying it would be easy. But you did make this venue, Campion. Surely it isn't beyond your immense capabilities to engineer a distraction."

"Flattery," I said, "will get you almost anywhere. But what about breaking into his ship? That won't exactly be child's play."

Purslane pressed a dainty finger to my lip. "I'll worry about the ship. You worry about the distraction."

We maintained our vigil on Burdock over the coming weeks, as our dangerous, delicious plan slowly came together. Burdock kept up the pattern of behaviour we had already noted, asking questions that probed the nature of the Great Work, but never directing his queries to known Advocates. More and more it seemed to us that there was something about the Work that had alarmed him; something too sensitive to bring to the attention of those who had a vested interest in the thing itself. But since Purslane and I were none the wiser about what the Great Work actually entailed, we could only guess about what it was that had unnerved Burdock. We both agreed that we needed to know more, but our suspicions about Burdock (and, by implication, Burdock's own suspicions) meant that we were just as incapable of putting direct questions to the Advocates. Day by day, therefore, I found myself making surreptitious enquires much like those made by Burdock himself. I endeavoured to target my questioning at different people than the ones Burdock had buttonholed, not wanting to spark anyone else's curiosity. Purslane did likewise, and—even as we planned our utterly illegal raid on Burdock's ship—we pieced together the tidbits of information we had gathered.

None of it was very illuminating, but by the same token little of it contradicted Purslane's conviction that the Great Work was related to the emergence of a single, Galaxy-spanning Supercivilisation. There were dark, glamorous rumours concerning the covert development of technologies that would bring this state of affairs into being.

I almost laughed. "We're immortal superbeings who've lived longer than some starfaring civilisations, including many Priors. If we choose, we can cross the Galaxy in the gap between thoughts. We can make worlds and shatter suns for our amusement. We can sip from the dreams and nightmares of fifty million billion sentient beings. Isn't that enough for you?"

"It might be enough for you and I, Campion. But then we've always had modest ambitions."

"But what about Burdock?" I asked. "He isn't linked to the Advocates, as far as I'm aware. I don't think he's been actively frozen out, but he certainly hasn't spent any time cultivating the right connections."

"I'll have to review the recordings again," Purslane said. "But I'm pretty sure none of his enquiries were directed at known Advocates. He was targeting people on the fringe: line members who might know something, without being directly privy to the big secret."

"Why wouldn't he just ask the Advocates directly?"

"Good question," Purslane said. "Of course, we could always ask *him*."

"Not until we know a bit more about what he's involved in."

"You know," Purslane said. "There's something else we could consider."

The tone of her voice prickled the hairs on the back of my neck. "I'm not going to like this, am I?"

"We could examine the records on his ship and find out what he was really up to."

"He's hardly likely to give us permission to do that."

"I wasn't talking about asking his permission." Purslane's smile was wicked and thrilling: she was actually enjoying our little adventure. "I was talking about going aboard and finding out for ourselves."

"Just like that, without so much as a by-your-leave?"

apart from that: at best they might have some vague knowledge of each other's existence, based on transmissions and data passed on by the likes of you and me. But what can two cultures on either side of the Galaxy know of each other? By the time one gets to hear about the other, the other probably doesn't exist any more. There's no possibility of mutual cooperation; the sharing of intellectual resources and knowledge." Purslane shrugged. "So those cultures stumble through the dark, making the same mistakes over and over again, constantly reinventing the wheel. At best they have some knowledge of galactic history, so they can avoid repeating the worst mistakes. At worst they're evolving in near-total ignorance. Some of them don't even remember how they got where they are."

I echoed Purslane's shrug. "But that's the way things must be. It's human nature for us to keep changing, to keep experimenting with new societies, new technologies, new modes of thought…"

"The very experiments that rip societies apart, and keep the wheel of history turning."

"But if we weren't like that, we wouldn't be human. Every culture in the Galaxy has the means to engineer itself into social stasis tomorrow, if the will were there. Some of them have probably tried it. But what's the point? We might stop the wheel of history turning, but we wouldn't be human anymore."

"I agree," Purslane said. "Meddling in human nature isn't the solution. But imagine if the intellectual capacity of the entire human Diaspora could somehow be tapped. At the moment those cultures are bumping around like random atoms in a gas. What if they could be brought into a state of coherence, like the atoms in a laser? Then there'd be real progress, with each achievement leading to the next. Then we could really start *doing* something."

THOUSANDTH NIGHT

"THIS IS THE third time that he's fished for information about the Great Work," Purslane said.

I nodded. On three occasions, Burdock had steered his conversations with other line members around to the subject of the Great Work. "He's very discrete about it," I said. "But you can tell he's itching to know more about it. But don't we all?"

"Not to that degree," she said. "I'm curious. I'd like to know what it is that has the lines so stirred up. But at the same time it doesn't keep me awake at night. I know that the secret will eventually be revealed. I'm patient enough to wait until then."

"Really?" I asked.

"Yes. And besides—I've heard enough rumours to think that I know half the answer already."

That was news to me. "Go on."

"It's about knitting the worlds of the lines into a cohesive entity—a Galactic Empire, if you like. At the moment such a thing clearly isn't practical. It takes us two hundred thousand years just to make one sweep through the Galaxy. That's much too long on a human scale. We might not experience much time passing in our ships, but that doesn't apply to the people living on planets. Entire cultures wax and wane while we're making course adjustments. Some of the people down on those planets have various forms of immortality, but that doesn't make history pass any less quickly. And it's history that keeps destroying things. It's history that stops us reaching our full potential."

"I'm not sure I follow you," I said.

"Think of all those myriad human cultures," Purslane said. "To all extents and purposes, they exist independently of each other. Those within a few light years of each other can exchange ideas and perhaps even enjoy a degree of trade. Most are too far day, and ran a simple program to isolate those instances where Burdock was talking to someone else or accessing data from one of the public nodes I'd dotted around the venue. I then took those isolated sequences and slipped them into Purslane's dreams, along with the allotted strand for that night. I did the same for myself: it meant that we had more to dream than everyone else, but that was a small price to pay.

By day, as we fulfilled our social obligations, we reviewed the Burdock data independently. The agreement was that if either of us noticed something unusual, we should leave a signal for the other party. Since I ran the venue, my signal consisted of a change to the patterning of the floor tiles on the thirtieth level terrazzo, cunningly encoding the time of the unusual event in the Burdock data. I'd been fiddling around with the patterns long before the Burdock affair, so there was nothing odd about my actions as far as anyone else was concerned. As for Purslane, she'd agreed to stand at noon at a certain position on one of my spray-lashed suspension bridges. By counting the number of wires between her and land, I could isolate the anomaly to within a few tens of minutes.

We'd agreed that we wouldn't meet in person until we'd had time to review each other's observations. If we agreed that there was something worth talking about, then we'd "accidentally" meet each other within the next few days. Then we'd judge the right moment to slip away to Purslane's ship. In practise, days and weeks would go by without Burdock doing anything that we both agreed was noteworthy or odd. Now and then he'd do or say something that hinted at a dark personal secret—but under that level of scrutiny, it was difficult to think of anyone who wouldn't. And who among us didn't have some secrets, anyway?

But by turns we noticed something that we couldn't dismiss.

"The environment doesn't report to me. It keeps this kind of thing to itself."

"But it could be programmed to report to you," Purslane said.

I squirmed. "Yes."

"I realise this is unorthodox, Campion. But I think we have to do it, given all that could be at stake."

"Burdock may say nothing."

"We won't know unless we try. How long would it take you to arrange this?"

"It's trivial," I admitted.

"Then do it. Last night was the eight hundred and third threading. There are less than two hundred days before we all leave Reunion. If we don't find out what Burdock's up to now, we may never have another chance." Purslane's eyes gleamed thrillingly. "We haven't a moment to lose."

PURSLANE AND I agreed that we should keep our meetings to a minimum from then on, in case we began to draw attention to ourselves. Liaisons between line members were normal enough—even long-term relationships—but the fact that we insisted on meeting out of the public eye was bound to raise eyebrows. Even given the absence of a single Secure anywhere in the venue, there were plenty of places that were private enough for innocent assignations.

But our assignation was anything but innocent.

It wasn't difficult to keep in touch, once we'd agreed a scheme. Since I had designed and constructed the venue, the machinery that handled the threading of the strands into our nightly dreams lay under my control. Each evening, I took the environment's covert observations of Burdock over the last including an embarrassing anecdote in a strand had almost become *de rigueur*.

"Maybe we should talk to Burdock," I said.

"What if we're wrong? If Burdock felt aggrieved, we could be ostracized by the entire line."

"It's a risk," I admitted. "But if he has done something bad, the line has to know about it. It would look very bad if one of the other lines discovered the truth before we did."

"Maybe we're making a mountain out of a molehill."

"Or maybe we're not. Could we force the issue out into the open somehow? What if you publicly accuse *me* of lying?"

"Risky, Campion. What if they believe me?"

"They won't be able to find any chinks in my story because there aren't any. After due process, the attention will shift to Burdock. If, as you said, there are other things in his strand that don't check out…"

"I don't like it."

"Me neither. But it's not as if I can think of any other way of pursuing this."

"There might be one," Purslane said, eyeing me cautiously. "You built these islands, after all."

"Yes," I allowed.

"Presumably it wouldn't stretch your talents to spy on Burdock."

"Oh, no," I said, shaking my head.

She raised a calming hand. "I don't mean putting a bug on him, following him to his ship, or anything like that. I just mean keeping a record of anything he does or says in public. Is your environment sophisticated enough to allow that?"

I couldn't lie. "Of course. It's constantly monitoring everything we do in public anyway, for our own protection. If someone has an accident…"

"So what's the problem?"

away any hint of the suspicion Purslane and I felt. At the same time my mind spun out of control with imagined crimes. Like any members of a starfaring society, those of Gentian Line had terrible powers at their disposal. One of our ships, used carelessly, could easily incinerate a world. Deliberate action was even more chilling to contemplate. Members of other lines *had* committed atrocities in the remote past. History was paved with genocides.

But nothing about Burdock suggested a criminal streak. He wasn't ambitious. His strands had always been unmemorable. He'd never attempted to influence Gentian policy. He had no obvious enemies.

"Do you think anyone else knows?" I asked Purslane, during another covert meeting aboard her ship. "After all, the evidence is all out there in the public realm. Anyone else could spot those discrepancies if they paid enough attention."

"That's the point, though: I don't think anyone else will. You and I are friends. I probably paid more attention to your sunsets than anyone else did. And I'm a stickler for detail. I've been looking out for false threads during every carnival."

"Because you suspected one of us might lie?"

"Because it made it more interesting."

"Maybe we're making too much of this," I said. "Maybe he just did something embarrassing that he wanted to cover up. Not a crime, but just something that would have made him look foolish."

"We've all done foolish things. That hasn't stopped any of us including them in our strands when the mood suits us. Remember Orpine, during the third carnival?"

Orpine had made a fool of herself near the Whipping Star, SS433, nearly crashing her ship in the process. But her honesty had endeared her to the rest of us. She had been chosen to forge the venue for the fourth carnival. Ever since then, were keeping an eye on us, sampling our strands, judging our wisdom and readiness.

Unofficially, there were also Gentian members who seemed to know something. I remembered Fescue's criticism of my strand: how there were turbulent times coming and how I'd have all the time in the world to loll around on beaches after the Great Work had been completed. Fescue—and a handful of other line members—had almost certainly been tipped off.

We called them the Advocates.

But while it seemed likely that we'd be invited to participate in the project before very long, we were also now at our most vulnerable. A single error could jeopardize our standing with the other lines. We'd all been mindful of this as we prepared our strands.

But what if one of us had done something truly awful? A crime committed by one Gentian Line member would reflect badly upon all of us. Technically, we were different manifestations of the same individual. If one Gentian member had it in them to do something bad, then it could be presumed that we all did.

If Burdock had indeed committed a crime, and if that crime came to light, then we might well be excluded from the Great Work.

"This could be bad," I said.

○←

IT WAS VERY hard to behave normally in the days and weeks that followed. No matter where I went, I bumped into Burdock with unerring regularity. Our paths had hardly crossed during this latest carnival, but now he and I seemed doomed to meet each other every day. During these awkward encounters I kept fumbling for the right tone, hoping that I never gave

"Anyone else?"

"Just you," Purslane said. "I'm worried, Campion. What if Burdock did something?"

"A crime?"

"It's not unthinkable."

But unthinkable was precisely what it was. Gentian Line was not the only one of its kind. When Abigail shattered herself, others had done likewise. Some of those lines had died out over the intervening time, but most had endured in some shape or form. Although customs varied, most of those lines had something similar to Reunion: a place where they convened and re-threaded memories.

In the last two million years there had been many instances of contact between those lines. Until recently Gentian Line had been isolationist, but some of the others had formed loose associations. There had been treaties and feuds. One entire line had been murdered, when a rival line booby-trapped its equivalent of Reunion with an antimatter device left over from the War of the Local Bubble. Nowadays we were all a lot more careful. There were formal ties between many of the lines. There were agreed rules of behaviour. Feuds were out, marriages were in. There were plans for future collaboration, like the Great Work.

The Great Work was a project—not yet initiated—which would require the active cooperation of many lines. Whatever it was was *big*. Beyond that I knew nothing about it. I wasn't alone in my ignorance. Officially, no members of Gentian Line were privy to detailed knowledge about the Great Work. That information was held by an alliance of lines to which we hadn't yet been granted full membership. The expectation, however, was that it wouldn't be long before we were invited into the club. Among the guests on Reunion were ambassadors from other lines—some of which were in on the big secret. They

"But his strand was threaded after mine. If he was going to lie…"

"I don't think he paid enough attention to your catalogue of sunsets," Purslane said. "Can't blame him, though, can you?"

"It could be me that's lying," I said.

"My money's still on Burdock. Anyway, that's not the only problem with his story. There are a couple of other glitches: nothing quite so egregious, but enough to make me pick through the whole thing looking for anomalies. That's when I spotted the contradiction."

I looked at her wonderingly. "This is serious."

"It could be."

"It must be. Harmless exaggeration is one thing. Even outright lying is understandable. But why would you replace the truth with something less interesting, unless you had something to hide?"

"That's what I thought as well."

"Why would he go to the trouble of creating an alibi, when he could just as easily delete the offending memories from his strand?"

"Risky," Purslane said. "Safer to swap the system he did visit with one in the same neck of the woods, so that it didn't throw his timings too far out, in case anyone dug too deeply into his strand."

"That doesn't help us work out where he was, though—the same neck of the woods still means hundreds of light years, thousands of possible systems."

"It's a big galaxy," said Purslane.

There was an uneasy silence. Far above us, beyond layers of armored metal, I heard the seismic groan as something colossal shifted and settled like a sleeping baby.

"Have you spoken to Burdock?"

"Not about this."

"But it happened?"

"Not exactly. But I think *something* happened to Burdock: something that had him doctoring his thread to create a false alibi."

I shifted in my seat. These were serious allegations, far above the usual bitchy speculation that attended any private discussion about other members of the Gentian Line. "How can you know?"

"Because his memories contradict yours. I know: I've checked. According to your mutual strands, the two of you should have both been in the same system at the same time."

"Which system?"

She told me. It was an unremarkable place: just another star dipping into an alien sea, as far as I was concerned. "I was there," I said. "But I definitely didn't bump into Burdock." I rummaged through my memories, digging through mnemonic headers to those specific events. "He didn't come nearby either. No interstellar traffic came close to that world during my entire stay. His ship might have been stealthed…"

"I don't think it was. Anyway, he doesn't mention you either. Was your ship stealthed?"

"No."

"Then he'd have seen you arriving or departing. The interstellar medium's pretty thick near there. Relativistic ships can't help but carve a wake through it. He'd surely have made some mention of that if the strand was real."

She was right. Accidental encounters were always celebrated: a triumph of coincidence over the inhuman scale of the Galaxy.

"What do you think happened?"

"I think Burdock was unlucky," Purslane said. "I think he picked that world out of a hat, never imagining you'd visit it just when he claimed to be there."

I didn't want to know, and I didn't ask.

"The point is delicate," Purslane said. "I could be wrong about it. I almost certainly am. After all, no one else seems to have noticed anything unusual..."

"Anything unusual about what?"

"Do you remember Burdock's thread?"

"Burdock? Yes, of course." It was a silly, if understandable question. None of us were capable of forgetting any of the threaded strands unless we made a conscious effort to delete them. "Not that there was much about it *worth* remembering." Burdock was a quiet, low-profile line member who never went out of his way to make a show of himself. He'd threaded his strand a few weeks earlier. It had been uneventful, and I hadn't paid much attention to it. "It was almost as if he was trying to upstage me in the dullness stakes."

"I think he lied," Purslane said. "I think Burdock's thread was deliberately altered."

"By Burdock himself?"

"Yes."

"Why would he do that, though? The strand still wasn't very interesting."

"I think that was the point. I think he wanted to conceal something that did happen. He used dullness as a deliberate camouflage."

"Wait," I said. "How can you be sure things just weren't that dull?"

"Because of a contradiction," Purslane said. "Look, when the last reunion ended we all of us hared off into the Galaxy in different directions. As far as I'm aware, none of us swapped plans or itineraries."

"Forbidden, anyway," I said.

"Yes. And the chances of any of us bumping into each other between then and now were tiny."

"If I wanted to make something up, don't you think I would have made it a tiny bit more exciting?"

"That's what I thought."

"Besides," I said. "I didn't *want* to win this time. Creating this venue was a major headache. You've no idea how much I agonised about the placement of these islands, let alone whatever I've cooked up for Thousandth Night."

"No, I can believe it. And I believe *you*. I just had to ask." She tugged down one of the spiral arms in her hair and bit on it nervously. "Though you could still be lying, I suppose."

"I'm not. Are you going to get to the point?"

My travel box had brought me into Purslane's hovering ship an hour after her departure. My ship was modestly sized for an interstellar craft; only three kilometers long, but Purslane's was enormous. It was two hundred kilometers from nose to tail, with a maximum width of twenty. The tail parts of her ship projected above the atmosphere, into the vacuum of space. By night they sparkled as anticollision fields intercepted and vaporised meteorites. Auroral patterns played around the upper extremities like a lapping tide.

There were many reasons why someone might need a ship this big. It might have been constructed around some antique but valuable moon-sized engine, or some huge, fabulously efficient prototype drive that no one else possessed. Any advance that could get you slightly closer to the speed of light was to be treasured. Or it might be that her ship carried some vast, secret cargo, like the entire sentient population of an evacuated planet. Or it might be that the ship had been made this big in a gesture of mad exuberance, simply because it was possible to do so. Or it might be—and here my thoughts choked on bitter alienness—that the ship had to be this big to contain its one living passenger. Purslane was human-sized now, but who was to say what her true form was like between our visits to Reunion?

"Come to torment me about sunsets?"

"Not exactly. You and I need to talk."

"We could always go to one of those exclusive orgies," I said teasingly.

"I mean somewhere private. *Very* private." She seemed distracted, quite unlike her usual self. "Did you create a Secure on this island?"

"I didn't see the need. I can create one, if you think it's worth it."

"No: that'll just draw too much attention. We'll have to make do with my ship."

"I really need to finish this bridge."

"Finish it. I'll be on my ship whenever you're ready."

"What is this about, Purslane?"

"Be on my ship."

She turned away. A few moments later a square glass pane tumbled out of the sky and lowered itself to the ground. Purslane stepped onto the pane. Its edges expanded and then angled upward to form a box. The box rose into the air, carrying Purslane, and then suddenly accelerated away from the island. I watched it speed into the distance, the grey light occasionally flaring off one of its flat sides. The box became tiny and then just a twinkling dot. It vanished into the scarred, mountainous hull of an enormous waiting ship.

I returned to my bridge-repair work, wondering.

"WHAT IS ALL this about?"

"It's about your thread, among other things." She looked at me astutely, reclining in the lounge chair that her ship had provided. "You told us all the truth, didn't you? You really did spend two hundred thousand years watching sunsets?"

into the nuclear structure of neutron stars, although no one had heard much from *them* lately. Against all this change, the nine hundred and ninety-three members of the Gentian Line must have appeared laughably quaint and antique, with our stolid adherence to traditional anatomy. But all this was just convention. Prior to arrival on the planet, we were free to adopt whatever forms we chose. The only rule was that when we emerged from our ships we must assume the forms of adult humans, and that we must bring our minds with us. Minor matters such as gender, build, pigmentation and sexual orientation were left to our discretion, but we were all obliged to carry the facial characteristics of Abigail Gentian: her high cheekbones, her strong jaw and the fact that her left eye was green and the other a wintery, jackdaw blue.

Everything else was up for grabs.

Perhaps it was the stirring up of the past as each new thread was added, but we all felt Abigail Gentian's base memories looming large in our thoughts as Thousandth Night approached. We remembered how it had felt to be just one individual, in the centuries before Abigail shattered herself into pieces and sent them roaming the Galaxy. We all remembered being Abigail.

Somewhere near the seven hundredth threading, I was again approached by Purslane. Her hair was styled in stiff spiral arms, like the structure of our galaxy. They twinkled with embedded gems: reds, yellows and hard blue-whites for different stellar populations.

"Campion?" she asked cautiously.

I turned from the balcony. I was repairing one of the bridges after a storm, knitting it back together with wizardlike hand movements, making the invisibly small machines that composed the bridge dance to my commands. Matter flowed like milk, and then hardened magically.

received that there'd been mutterings that I must have spiced things up for effect. I hadn't—those things really had happened to me—but I'd still spent the rest of the reunion in a state of prickly self-defence.

It was better now. I enjoyed feeling my mind filling with bright new experience; multiple snapshots of a dizzying complex and teeming Galaxy. It was the euphoria of drunkenness combined with an absolute, crystalline clarity of mind. It was glorious and overwhelming: an avalanche of history.

At the last count there were ten million settled solar systems out there. Fifty million planet-class worlds. Entire upstart civilisations had risen and fallen since the last reunion, several times over. With the passing of every reunion it seemed impossible that the wilder fringes of humanity could become any stranger, any less recognizable. Yet they always contrived to do so; oozing into every cosmic niche like molten lava, and then carving out new niches that no one had dared dreamed of before.

Two million years of bioengineering and cyborg reshaping had equipped humankind for any possible physical environment. Twenty thousand distinct branches of humanity had returned to alien seas, each adopting a different solution to the problem of aquatic life. Some were still more or less humanoid, but others had sculpted themselves into sleek shark-like things, or dextrous multi-limbed molluscs or hard-shelled arthropods. There were thirteen hundred distinct human cultures in the atmospheres of gas giants. Ninety that swam in the metallic hydrogen oceans under those atmospheres. There were vacuum dwellers and star dwellers. There were people who lived in trees, and people who had, by some definition, become trees themselves. There were people as large as small moons, which fostered entire swarming communities within their bodies. There were people who had encoded themselves

"But you didn't tell me it was *this* exclusive," I said.

Purslane disrobed. As they stepped away, her clothes assumed the texture of weathered stone and froze into sculptural forms from deep antiquity. "Are you complaining?" she asked.

My own clothes broke up into a cloud of cherry blossom petals and scudded away across the floor. "Not exactly, no."

Purslane looked on approvingly. "I can tell."

We rolled around on the glass floor, which softened and hardened itself in perfect consideration of our needs. As we made love, I tried to remember whether I'd designed the glass floor to be transparent in both directions—and if so what kind of entertainment we were providing to the line members who might be looking up to the fiftieth floor from below. Then I decided that I didn't care. If we outraged them, so be it.

"You were right," Purslane said, when we were lying together afterwards.

"Right about what?"

"The sunsets. Every bit as…challenging…as you said."

"Go on. Kick a man when he's down."

"Actually I admire your nerve," she said. "You had a plan and you stuck with it. And some of the sunsets were actually quite nice."

She'd meant it as a compliment, but I couldn't help looking wounded. "Quite nice."

Purslane conjured a grape and popped it into my mouth. "Sorry, Campion."

"It's all right," I said. "At least I won't have people pestering me for the rest of the carnival, trying to get at the memories I edited out of the strand. At least they'll know that's precisely as exciting as it gets."

It was true: the pressure was off, and to my surprise I actually started relaxing and enjoying the remaining days and nights. The last time, my submitted strand had been so well

"That's different. We have duties…obligations. Purslane wouldn't understand that. She had her chance to join us."

"If you've got something to say, why not say it to her face?"

He looked away, to the brush-thin line of the horizon. "You did well with the aquatics," he said absently. "Nice touch. Mammals. They're from…*the old place*, aren't they?"

"I forget. What is this little pep talk about, Fescue? Are you telling me to keep away from Purslane?"

"I'm telling you to buck up your ideas. Start showing some *spine*, Campion. Turbulent times are coming. Admiring sunsets is all very well, but what we need now is hard data on emergent cultures across the entire Galaxy. We need to know who's with us and who isn't. There'll be all the time in the world for lolling around on beaches after we've completed the Great Work." Fescue poured the remains of his wine into my ocean. "Until then we need a degree of focus."

"Focus yourself," I said, turning away.

THINGS BEGAN TO improve in the afternoon, when interest shifted to the next evening's strand. Purslane found me again, attending to a whimsical redesign of one of the outlying towers. She told me that she had heard about an orgy on the fiftieth level of the main spire, very exclusive, and that I should join her there in an hour. Still stinging from Fescue's criticism, I told her that I was in no mood for it, but Purslane won me over and I agreed to meet when I was done with the tower.

When I arrived, the only other person there was Purslane.

"Wrong floor, I take it?"

"No," she said, standing on the perfectly transparent floor of an out-flung balcony, so that she appeared to float two kilometers above the sea. "Right floor, right time. I told you it was exclusive."

"Yes, actually. Aren't you?"

"It's not a matter of enjoyment. Not for some us, at any rate. There's work to be done during these reunions—serious business, of great importance to the future status of the line."

"Lighten up," I said under my breath.

Fescue and I had never seen eye to eye. Among the nine hundred and ninety-three surviving members of the line, there were two or three dozen who exerted special influence. Though we had all been created at the same time, these figures had cultured a quiet superiority, distancing themselves from the more frivolous aspects of a reunion. Their body plans and clothes were studiedly formal. They spent a lot of time standing around in grave huddles, shaking their heads at the rest of us. They had the strongest ties to external lines. Many of them were Advocates, like Fescue himself.

If Fescue had heard my whispered remark, he kept it to himself. "I saw you with Purslane earlier," he said.

"It's not against the law."

"You spend a lot of time with her."

"Again…whose business is it? Just because she turned her nose up at your elitist little club."

"Careful, Campion. You've done well with this venue, but don't overestimate your standing. Purslane is a troublemaker—a thorn in the line."

"She's my friend."

"That's clear enough."

I bristled. "Meaning what?"

"I didn't see either of you at the orgy this morning. You spend a lot of time together, just the two of you. You sleep together, yet you disdain sexual relationships with the rest of your fellows. That isn't how we like to do things in Gentian Line."

"You Advocates keep yourselves to yourselves."

"What's it going to be? You can't do a Cloud Opera, if that's what you've planned. We had one of those last time."

"Not a very good one though."

"And the time before that—what was it?"

"A recreation of a major space battle, I think. Effective, if a little on the brash side."

"Yes, I remember now. Didn't Fescue's ship mistake it for a real battle? Dug a ten kilometer wide crater into the crust when his screens went up. The silly fool had his defence thresholds turned down too low." Unfortunately, Fescue was in earshot. He looked at us over the shoulder of the line member he was talking to, shot me a warning glance then returned to his conversation. "Anyway," Samphire continued, oblivious. "What do you mean, you can't wait? It's your show, Campion. Either you've planned something or you haven't."

I looked at him pityingly. "You've never actually won best strand, have you?"

"Come close, though...my strand on the Homunculus Wars..." He shook his head. "Never mind. What's your point?"

"My point is that sometimes the winner elects to suppress their memories of exactly what form the Thousandth Night celebrations will take."

Samphire touched a finger to his nose. "I know you, Campion. It'll be tastefully restrained...and very, very dull."

"Good luck with your strand," I said icily.

Samphire left me. I thought I'd have a few moments alone, but no sooner had I turned to admire the view than Fescue leaned against the balustrade next to me, swilling a glass of wine. He held the glass by the stem, in jewelled and ringed fingers.

"Enjoying yourself, Campion?" he asked, in his usual deep voiced, paternalistic, faintly disapproving way. The wind flicked iron-grey hair from his aristocratic brow.

THOUSANDTH NIGHT

THAT NIGHT MY memories were threaded into the dreams of the other guests. Come morning most of them managed to say something vaguely complimentary about my strand, but beneath the surface politeness their bemused disappointment was all too obvious. It wasn't just that my memories had added nothing startling to the whole. What really annoyed them was that I'd apparently gone out of my way to have as dull a time as possible. The implication was that I'd let the side down by looking for pointless green flashes rather than adventure; that I'd deliberately sought to add nothing useful to the tapestry of our collective knowledge.

By the afternoon, my patience was wearing perilously thin.

"Well, at least you won't be on the edge of your seat come Thousandth Night," said Samphire, an old acquaintance in the line. "That *was* the idea, wasn't it?"

"I'm sorry?"

"Deliberate dullness, to take you out of the running for best strand."

"That wasn't the idea at all," I said testily. "Still, if you think it was dull…that's your prerogative. When's your strand, Samphire? I'll be sure to offer my heartfelt congratulations when everyone else is sticking the boot in."

"Day eight hundred," he said easily. "Plenty of time to study the opposition and make a few judicious alterations." Samphire sidled a bit too close for comfort. I had always found Samphire cloying, but I tolerated his company because his strands were usually memorable. He had a penchant for digging through the ruins of ancient human cultures, looting their tombs for quaint technologies, grisly weapons, and machine minds driven psychotic by two million years of isolation. "So anyway," he said, conspiratorially. "Thousandth Night. *Thousandth Night.* Can't wait to see what you've got lined up for us."

"Nor can I."

himself in always end up making him look wonderful, and everyone else a bit thick?"

"True. This time even his usual admirers have been tut-tutting behind his back."

"Serves him right."

Purslane looked out to sea, through the thicket of hovering ships parked around the tight little archipelago. A layer of cloud had formed during the afternoon, with the ships—most of them stationed nose down—piercing it like daggers. There were nearly a thousand of them. The view resembled an inverted landscape: a sea of fog, interrupted by the sleek, luminous spires of tall buildings.

"Asphodel's ship still hasn't been sighted," Purslane said. "It's looking as if she won't make it."

"Do you think she's dead?"

Purslane dipped her head. "I think it's a possibility. That last strand of hers...a lot of risk-taking."

Asphodel's strand, delivered during the last reunion, had been full of death-defying sweeps past lethal phenomena. What had seemed beautiful then—a whiplashing binary star, or a detonating nova—must have finally reached out and killed her. Killed one of *us*.

"I liked Asphodel," I said absently. "I'll be sorry if she doesn't make it. Maybe she's just delayed."

"Why don't you come inside and stop moping?" Purslane said, edging me away from the balcony. "It's not good for you."

"I'm not really in the mood."

"Honestly, Campion. I'm sure you're going to startle us tonight."

"That depends," I said, "on how much you like sunsets."

Purslane fixed me with a knowing smile. Her hair was bunched and high, sculpted like a fairytale palace with spires and turrets. "Typical false modesty." She pushed a glass of red wine into my hand before I could refuse.

"Well, this time there's nothing false about it. My thread is going to be a crashing anti-climax. The sooner we get over it, the better."

"It's going to be that dull?"

I sipped at the wine. "The very exemplar of dullness. I've had a spectacularly uneventful two hundred thousand years."

"You said exactly the same thing last time, Campion. Then you showed us wonders and miracles. You were the hit of the reunion."

"Maybe I'm getting old," I said, "but this time I felt like taking things a little bit easier. I made a conscious effort to keep away from inhabited worlds; anywhere there was the least chance of something exciting happening. I watched a lot of sunsets."

"Sunsets," she said.

"Mainly solar-type stars. Under certain conditions of atmospheric calm and viewing elevation you can sometimes see a flash of green just before the star slips below the horizon..." I trailed off lamely, detesting the sound of my own voice. "All right. It's just scenery."

"Two hundred thousand years of it?"

"I'm not repentant. I enjoyed every minute of it."

Purslane sighed and shook her head: I was her hopeless case, and she didn't mind if I knew it. "I didn't see you at the orgy this morning. I was going to ask what you thought of Tormentil's strand."

Tormentil's memories, burned into my mind overnight, still had an electric brightness about them. "The usual self-serving stuff," I said. "Ever noticed that all the adventures he embroils

In little over a year machines would pulverise the islands, turning their spired buildings into powdery rubble. The sea would have pulled them under by the time the last of our ships had left the system. But even the sea would only last a few thousand years after that. I'd steered water-ice comets onto this arid world just to make its oceans. The atmosphere itself was dynamically unstable. We could breathe it now, but there was no biomass elsewhere on Reunion to replenish the oxygen we were turning into carbon dioxide. In twenty thousand years the world would be uninhabitable to all but the hardiest microorganisms. It would stay like that for the better part of another hundred and eighty thousand years, until our return.

By then the scenery would be someone else's problem, not mine. On Thousandth Night—the final evening of the reunion—the person who had threaded the most acclaimed strand would be charged with designing the venue for the next gathering. Depending on their plans, they'd arrive between one thousand and ten thousand years before the official opening of the next gathering.

My hand tightened on the rail at the edge of the high balcony as I heard urgent footsteps approach from behind. High hard heels on marble, the swish of an evening gown.

"Don't tell me, Campion. Nerves."

I turned around, greeting Purslane—beautiful, regal Purslane—with a stiff smile and a grunt of acknowledgement. "Mm. How did you guess?"

"Intuition," she said. "Actually, I'm surprised you're here at all."

"Why's that?"

"When it's my turn I'm sure I'll still be on my ship, furiously re-editing until the last possible moment."

"That's the problem," I said. "I've done all the editing I need. There's nothing *to* edit. Nothing of any consequence has happened to me since the last time."

THOUSANDTH NIGHT

I T WAS THE AFTERNOON before my threading, and stomach butterflies were doing their best to unsettle me. I had little appetite and less small talk. All I wanted was for the next twenty-four hours to slip by so that it could be someone else's turn to sweat. Etiquette forbade it, but there was nothing I'd have preferred than to flee back to my ship and put myself to sleep until morning. Instead I had to grin and bear it, just as everyone else had to when their night came around.

Waves crashed a kilometer below, dashing against the bone-white cliffs, the spray cutting through one of the elegant suspension bridges that linked the main island to the smaller ones surrounding it. Beyond the islands, the humped form of an aquatic crested the waves. I made out the tiny dots of people frolicking on the bridge, dancing in the spray. It had been my turn to design the venue for this carnival, and I thought I'd made a tolerable job of it.

A pity none of it would last.

Thousandth Night and Minla's Flowers Copyright © 2009 by Alastair Reynolds. All rights reserved.

"Thousandth Night" Copyright © 2007 by Alastair Reynolds, first appeared in *One Million A.D.*, edited by Gardner Dozois. All rights reserved.

Dust jacket illustration Copyright © 2009 by Tomislav Tikulin. All rights reserved.

Interior design Copyright © 2009 by Desert Isle Design, LLC. All rights reserved.

First Edition

ISBN
978-1-59606-259-7

Subterranean Press
PO Box 190106
Burton, MI 48519

www.subterraneanpress.com

THOUSANDTH NIGHT

ALASTAIR REYNOLDS

SUBTERRANEAN PRESS • 2009

THOUSANDTH NIGHT

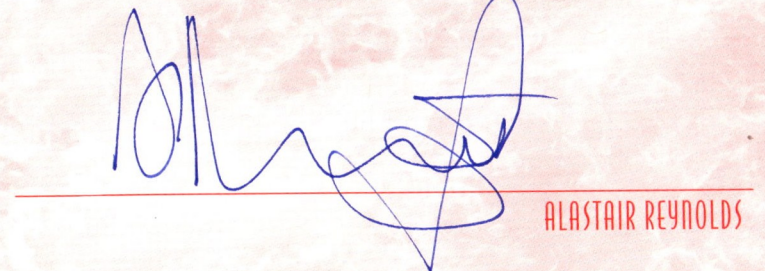